When Magnolias Bloom

Written by G.L. Gracie

When Magnolias Bloom
By G.L. Gracie
© 2015 Published by G.L. Gracie
Formatting and Graphics by Leah Banicki

https://www.facebook.com/G.L.Gracie

1

Somewhere Outside Washington, D.C.
Spring, 1864

Chase

Sounds of coach wheels churning against the muddy road made a grinding noise which seemed to penetrate the very souls of its passengers. All was quiet except for those sounds and those of the driver as he whipped the horses over the rutted roadway. Mud splashed up through the space near the bottom of the door. A small girl sitting across from him kept an eye on the ooze while she clutched at a doll with a china head and frilly dress, not unlike the ones his sister had played with as a child. The youngster sat next to a woman he surmised was the little girl's mother. On the other side of her was an older woman who frequently dozed off in the stifling heat which continued to persist in the confines of the coach. From what he had observed, the three were traveling together and the older woman possibly was the grandmother. Sitting next to him was a rather stern looking man reading a rather worn book. Chase was the fifth passenger in the coach. He wondered what destination occupied each person's mind. Certainly none of the other passengers were taking as long or as treacherous a journey as the one he was embarking upon.

Indeed, Chase Stewart was probably the only passenger in this coach who had something to hide. Feeling the cold blade of the knife against his leg gave him a feeling of security, but also a feeling of apprehension at what he might encounter in the weeks to come. The pistol he carried in his baggage would remain there until he was farther south. Money belts were strategically strapped in various places on his body as well as in concealed compartments in the tapestry bag which held his only belongings. Perhaps its contents were too sparse for this trip, but he needed to travel light; and much thinking and preparation had gone into the selection of items that would be most valuable to earn a place in the bag.

He winked at the little girl who immediately moved closer to her mother, clutched her doll to her chest and avoided his eyes. He smiled. Not trusting. That was probably a good quality in these days of turmoil. It was difficult to know who one could trust with all the unrest and the confusion of politics and secrecy. How the world had turned upside down these past few years!

Why, just four years ago, the Stewart family had been content and happy in their three story home in Washington, D. C., living the affluent life when the biggest concern was whether or not one should go into the office for the day or take the day off or perhaps make a decision about whether or not the evening meal would be beef or chicken. Actually, mother made the food choices and then informed the servants of their duties. At least she had until the last year or so. Father handled the business concerns and Chase was pretty much carefree.

There were three boys in the Stewart household. Chase was the youngest son of Sylvester Stewart and Claudia Louise Chase Stewart. Mother was the daughter of a business financier and father was in the law business and dabbled a bit in politics. Chase's oldest brother, Clinton, was in business with father and had married into wealth. It turned out that brother Edward fancied the import business...and beautiful young women. And young women and some who were slightly older fancied Edward, too. Edward had definitely managed to get the good looks in the family. But Edward was fun to be around, not stodgy like Clinton, so Edward and Chase had many good times together. But not as many times as the two younger Stewart children. After having three boys, the Stewarts had been blessed with a daughter, Samantha. There being only one year difference in their ages, Chase and Samantha had been close right from the very beginning.

The third part of their threesome was neighbor and good friend, Nathan Clevenger. Nathan lived several blocks away from the Stewart household and any one of the three was seldom seen without the other two. Nathan and Chase were the same age and along with Samantha, they were almost inseparable…and unstoppable in their antics. Chase had always thought Samantha would grow up to marry Nathan and indeed there was a deep connection there. But things had changed dramatically in the past few years.

Father had seen fit to pay the price to keep Clinton and Edward and Chase from participating in the war just when Chase and his friend, Nathan, were considering enlisting. Nathan had left with the union troops while Chase had stayed behind. Although he was temporarily discouraged by father's decision, he now had a more important mission…and one that was equally as exciting and equally as dangerous.

With everyone else in the family engaged in business and since Chase and Samantha were so very close, it only made sense that he be the one to make the journey.

How long had it been since he'd seen his little sister? Four years now? Right after her wedding day. And hadn't she been beautiful in her wedding dress that day in July?

His throat constricted as he remembered the scene. Fresh flowers had been added to the gardens. A pleasant summer day greeted the assembled guests, all dressed in their finery. Although the time had been short to make the preparations, mother had worked magic in creating the perfect wedding for her only daughter. Chase had been part of the wedding party so he had full view of his little sister, Samantha, as she glided through the crowd of well-wishers on her way to meet her confederate groom. She was enveloped in yards and yards of white fabric cut so her shoulders were exposed, the most exclusive gown money could buy. Pink roses tucked in her dark curls matched the ones she carried in her hands; and when she came close enough to him, he could see the happiness in her green eyes and the love she felt for the southern gentleman waiting for her at the altar.

Looking beyond Samantha, Chase could see the face of his friend, Nathan, and saw the sadness in his eyes. Yes, Nathan would have been Chase's choice for his little sister.

But the dashing Grady Reynolds had come to Washington from the south on business in behalf of his plantation and his path had crossed with that of brother Edward. In the short time they had known each other, the two had become friends and Edward had invited Grady to the Stewart household for dinner. It was under those circumstances that Grady and Samantha met and the whirlwind of plans and activities begun. Although she was only seventeen years old, twenty five year old Grady had proposed marriage and plans had been made. The sound of her voice still echoed in his ears.

"Oh, Chase," she chirped. "Isn't he the handsomest?"

"I guess."

"He is! No doubt about it. Are you blind?"

He tried to ignore her exuberance.

"Are you sure, Samantha? Really sure?" he persuaded. "You've only known each other a short time."

"I couldn't be more sure of anything in my entire life," she swooned.

"But you've always been impetuous and you'll be such a long distance from us...from me," he was saddened.

"It won't be that far. And he says the plantation house is rather large. You all can come for a visit. There are horses a plenty for riding and elegant parties, I'm sure."

"Still..." Chase objected. "You are easily taken in. Life is about more than riding horses and elegant parties."

Samantha and Chase walked together through the fragrant gardens of their family home. It was a comfortable place with flowers and shrubs and hedges and benches for sitting and fountains that bubbled up and overflowed concrete bowls, far away from the seamier side of Washington. The three story house that loomed behind the gardens glistened in the sun. It was immaculate in every way with its arches and scroll work and kept in great condition by several servants. A cook and house maids took care of domestic things while a footman and butler and gardener took care of other matters.

"Are you jealous?" she turned to him. "That's it. You are jealous!"

"Well, maybe," he said seriously. "We've always been together. We've never been apart."

It was true. The brother and sister had been inseparable since they were toddlers in the house nursery. Skinned knees and pranks and hours of play had given them a strong bond. Often father had commented that what one didn't think of, the other did. And Chase was unsure how he felt about that bond being broken.

Chase, the son named for his mother's family, stood head and shoulders above her, trim and handsome and full of vitality. His dark brown hair, the same color as their mother's hair, was slicked back from his face which was always clean shaven. He had an athletic build and was always happy and positive. Indeed, there was nothing that seemed impossible in their world of youth.

Looking up into Chase's blue eyes...the ones that always twinkled with mischief...she felt the twinge of separation. They often joked about knowing each other's feelings; and this was one of those times Samantha sensed his sadness. Taking him by the arm, she walked beside him.

"You're the best brother ever," she said softly. "And I will miss you terribly. But I want you to be happy for me."

"Oh, I want you to be happy," he patted her arm in his. "It's not about that. It's just that South Carolina is such a long way away and I will long to see you."

He paused.

"But I know that Grady makes you happy. I've seen that in your face."

"You will come visit me then, won't you?" she begged.

"Of course. The strongest storm could not keep me from you," he promised.

———————— ⌒◯◯⌒ ————————

The storm that came happened in April of 1861 when the south decided to secede from the union. No one had counted on that, at least in the happy secure world of the Stewart family. It seemed as if Samantha and Grady had no more than left Washington amid a crowd of family and friends wishing health and prosperity for the newlyweds than news of the war broke out. And daily reports coming from the front lines were not encouraging. Tales of horror and panic and devastation ran rampant.

Chase twisted in his seat as he thought of the possibilities. Perhaps he should have tried to dissuade Samantha from marrying Grady and moving to South Carolina. Although unrest in the south had been rumored for months before the actual attack, it hadn't been taken all that seriously by the Stewart family. Now they were directly affected. A prayer passed over his lips as he thought once more about his little sister who had been gone so long from the family. At any rate, he hoped Grady Reynolds was protecting his little sister, that she was safe and out of harm's way.

She had written to him. He kept the letter and read it over and over again, committing her words to memory. He dared not bring it with him. A union man traveling through the south with such a letter might have his mission misconstrued. But he knew every word by heart and he repeated them often in his mind. Settling back against the jostling coach seat, he closed his eyes as he recalled the letter and the smell of her perfume.

My dearest Chase,

I miss you terribly, but Hummingbird Hill is a beautiful place. I want for nothing other than the company of my dear family for which I yearn.

I have many hands here to help me. We had paid servants

in Washington, but here I am attended by black slaves. I do not know yet if I am comfortable with that situation, but Grady tells me the plantation cannot survive without their labor.

I am learning new things each day and Grady makes me very happy.

Come visit me soon. Come in the spring of the year. It is particularly lovely here when the magnolias are in bloom.

Your loving sister,
Samantha

The rest of the letter gave specific instructions for travel from Washington to the plantation in South Carolina. Again, he went over the information in his head. No way could he carry something as valuable as this anywhere but in his head.

Mother had been beside herself when the news reports came in from the south...Fort Sumter had been attacked; and although Samantha lived on the other side of the state, Claudia Chase Stewart shuddered with the thought that her beloved daughter might be in danger. As a matter of fact, it had affected her already questionable health; and quite often these days she had taken to her bed. Father labored over the reports as well but kept his thoughts to himself, not willing to further upset his wife. But he could no longer ignore the fact that Samantha might well be in danger or that his beloved wife was suffering so much not knowing of her daughter's wellbeing. So it was that Father had seen fit to call Chase aside. Chase knew something was up when he saw both of his brothers summoned to the family library as well.

"*Am I in trouble here?*" *he asked upon seeing the seriousness on the faces of the three men he saw seated before him.*

His remark was not met with smiles. Chase immediately knew this was not merely a chastisement for one of his escapades. This was serious business.

Father started the dialogue.

"*I've been very concerned about Samantha since this insanity has broken out,*" *he began.* "*We all have been. And I know you are aware that your mother's illness is a major concern. I would not want her to...*"

Here Sylvester Stewart's words faltered.

"*I want her to be reunited with Samantha before...well, you understand.*"

Sylvester Stewart gestured towards his two older sons as if he needed their help to make his point.

Chase turned to study the faces of his two brothers...Clinton with his paleness and spectacles and seriousness, Edward with his handsome face and boyish charm.

"*Conditions have worsened in the south,*" *Clinton volunteered.* "*This war is dragging on with no end in sight.*"

"*It's bad,*" *Edward added.*

"*How bad?*" *he heard himself saying, trying desperately to ignore the pain that suddenly developed in his stomach.*

His father continued.

"*Plantations have been raided and burned. We are concerned about Samantha and her safety. Although we believe she is not in the thick of the fighting, we are still worried and think someone should go down there and ...well, see if she is alright...bring her back here to her family...to her mother.*"

Sylvester Stewart choked again with emotion.

It took a moment before Chase put things together in his mind. Looking into the eyes of his brothers, the scenario began to play in his head. First, Clinton. He was the oldest but he wouldn't be the one to go. He was in the law firm and had a new wife and a baby on the way. Absently, he looked at Edward. No, not Edward. Edward had more than he could handle with supplying materials to the war effort. The realization hit him that he indeed had been the one chosen for the job. Was it even possible? Could such a thing even be accomplished?

"The best plan of action seems to be a man traveling alone should have the best chance of breaking through any military line and of skirting any battles. It will require a lot of endurance and skill, son," his father was saying. "I've thought it through. I do not wish to put another of my family in danger. You will be at the mercy of all kinds of trials along the way. But I think you can do it, son."

The last words were accompanied by a slap on Chase's shoulder. His father meant it as a sign of encouragement and faith in him. Instead, Chase felt the weight of responsibility descend on his shoulders, the same weight that remained there to this day. But Chase would do anything for his little sister; and if Sylvester Stewart had said it should be done, then he would do it.

For some reason the horses chose this moment to veer from their course, the coach shifted and Chase changed positions in the seat. This would be the easy part of the trip. There was a long trail up ahead, some 500 miles to Hummingbird Hill and Samantha. Probably after today he would be traveling undercover of nightfall and by horseback. He looked out the small window next to him and watched the countryside pass by.

2

Four Years Earlier, York County, South Carolina
1860

Samantha

"Thank you, Elijah," Samantha said as she took the reins from Elijah's weathered hands.

"Yes, 'um," came the humble reply as he nodded his graying head.

But Elijah hesitated.

Taking notice of Elijah's uneasiness, Samantha looked down at him from her place perched on the roan colored horse that had become hers since her arrival at Hummingbird Hill. The roan danced in place, eager to be on his way.

"What is it, Elijah?" she asked.

Elijah dropped his eyes and stared at the ground.

"Elijah, if you have something to say, just say it," she appeared to be annoyed.

"Well, missus," he faltered, "iz you sure you want ta ride rather then take the buggy?"

"Is that all? Of course, I'm sure. It's a beautiful day for a ride and I love the feeling of being on horseback."

When Elijah's eyes met hers, she saw what she perceived to be fear in them.

"Are you thinking you will be in trouble for the choice I've made?"

Elijah hung his head once again in silence.

Samantha knew Elijah to be a good man, a gentle man, an elderly man, the husband of Callie, the plantation cook. Their children...Moses, Aaron and Miriam...named for those heroes in the Bible...were also slaves on the plantation. His hair was turning white with the years he'd spent at Hummingbird Hill. Elijah had been purchased in the early years by Grady's father and now he faithfully served Grady himself. He no longer worked the fields, but cared for the stable and the horses with love and concern. The horses reflected his gentleness.

"Don't worry," she encouraged. "I'll handle it if anything is said."

With that, she nudged the roan and left the stable area, heading for the ridge above the Catawba. From there she could see the magnificent rolling current of the river in one direction and overlook the cotton fields in the other. York County was comprised of mostly small farms thus making Hummingbird Hill unique. It was quite possibly the largest plantation in this part of the state and rivaled those in many other areas of the south.

And this particular place...this place on the bluff where she loved to come...offered a spectacular view of Hummingbird Hill with its impressive house and outbuildings and gardens. As well as the cotton fields for income, the plantation was pretty much self-sufficient with its large gardens of every kind of vegetable and hogs for butchering and chickens and geese and ducks and several head of cattle for milk cows and beef. It took a lot of food to supply all of the people residing at Hummingbird Hill. Grady had not exaggerated one bit in his description of life in the northern part of South Carolina. The house was magnificent and the scenery breathtaking. She had not wanted for anything since her arrival...not anything but the comfort of her family and life back in Washington.

Cautioning herself against the melancholy thoughts of home could bring to her, she instead let the spring breeze play with her dark locks of hair and inhaled the smell of mock orange which bloomed near the river's edge.

This part of South Carolina...this up country as it was called...was a lush vacation spot for wealthy plantation owners from down state. Resorts were nestled among the rolling hills and provided a nice reprieve for those from the low country.

Seventeen had been a very young age to take over the management of such a large household staff. As mistress of the plantation, it was her responsibility to see to the wellbeing of the slaves. Mostly she got along well with the coloreds although Grady constantly told her they could not be *given an inch* as he put it. She kept his words in the back of her head, but alongside his words were those of her father. *Treat people in the way you would want to be treated and they will respond to your kindness.*

Father's philosophy worked well with Callie, the head cook over the kitchen help and with Samantha's personal young maid, Izzy. It had not worked well with the mean-spirited Clover. Clover's eyes were evil and Samantha was often puzzled by that. She sensed resentment in Clover. Clover was a large boned woman probably in her mid-twenties in age and assigned to house work, possibly chosen for the position because of her natural athletic ability. Indeed, Clover was strong and could move heavy pieces of furniture as well as any man even though she had delivered a child right after Samantha's arrival and was indeed again pregnant with what Samantha thought was her fourth child. But she *was* a good worker and she did keep the house clean and in order.

No matter how kind Samantha tried to be to Clover, she was met with a clear disregard of respect. Of course it was not blatant or Clover's position would have been in jeopardy. Perhaps Grady was right when he told Samantha it must be her imagination. Still, Samantha kept a strict eye out whenever Clover was around.

The trip from Samantha's home in Washington, D. C. to the plantation had been a glorious one. Grady was clever and entertaining and attentive. Somehow that had changed when they arrived at Hummingbird Hill. Samantha couldn't put her finger on it, but he seemed to be more focused on things other than Samantha, distancing himself from her. And of course, he had obligations to make the plantation run smoothly. But, as mistress of the plantation, she had her own set of duties as well. The health of the slaves was her responsibility. Keeping the darkies healthy meant a stronger work force so any health issue needed to be reported to Samantha and she swiftly learned the standard treatments for various conditions. She also learned very quickly which slaves were apt to pretend illness in order to get out of work. And all this information was kept in a small ledger Grady had provided.

She ran the household, keeping track of supplies and costs. She supervised the household staff. Planning for social events and entertaining were her responsibility. Yes, Samantha had plenty to keep her busy. Grady's lack of tenderness was just something she had to deal with.

Thoughts of her life in Washington caused her to wish she could talk to Nathan Clevenger about how she felt. He always seemed to understand her and cheer her. She had written to him as soon as she arrived in South Carolina. Perhaps Nathan and Chase would come visit her. How wonderful that would be! The three of them together again.

The big roan began to dance, having been stabled for too long, so Samantha urged him forward and together they flew over the countryside. After he'd had a good run and some of his restlessness satisfied, she pulled him to a walk near the cotton fields.

Crops had been good and Grady was pleased. All in all, Samantha's first year at Hummingbird Hill had been a good experience. There had been parties to host and Grady's friends to meet and shopping excursions to purchase things for the house or new gowns for her personal use. He had even taken her on a trip across the state to Charleston where he had indulged her with food delicacies and fine dress shops. He commissioned a huge painting to be made of Samantha and now it hung in the front hallway of the mansion. And all of it was due to the fields of cotton spread out before her.

She'd been reminded of that often enough.

Maybe this restlessness within her was a normal thing. Perhaps if she ignored it, it would go away.

The darkies were planting now and she could see them in the fields, the small children playing near their working parents. She was saddened by the fact that very soon those small children would be expected to work alongside their parents. But Grady said that was as it should be. He had rebelled at her idea of starting a school for them. He kept record books on all the babies born in the slave cabins because he said they were assets. The more babies, the more workers; and any baby born on the plantation became the property of the plantation owner, increased his worth.

Suddenly her attention was caught by the arrival of Hardy, the overseer for the plantation. He was coming toward the cotton fields on horseback at a terrifically fast pace towards the group of slaves working in the field some distance in front of her. A wise Samantha scanned the field to see what had provoked the overseer. All she saw were black slaves toiling away planting cotton. Suddenly, Hardy pulled out his whip and struck one of the workers around the back and shoulders. She flinched in the saddle. What had caused that course of action? Becoming aware of what was taking place before her, she was very conscious that no one came to the injured man's aid; and in fact, the action seemed to be completely ignored by the others working in the field. The beaten man returned to his work while Hardy waved his whip over his head and shouted some words that were indistinguishable to her as he spurred his horse forward towards another field.

As the overseer moved on, Samantha urged the roan down to the road where she could get a closer look. Blood stained the back of the worker's shirt but he kept planting as did the others. No one acknowledged her as Samantha walked the roan beside the field. Shirtless men revealed scars across their backs, some of which were not even healed yet.

There was something about Hardy that repelled Samantha. She didn't know if it was the way he treated the slaves or because he drank to excess or because her skin crawled when he looked at her. Grady said Hardy was just doing what was expected of him and there was nothing for her to be concerned about. But, like Sylvester Stewart had taught his daughter, there were some people you just needed to avoid.

Later that evening, after dinner dishes had been cleared away and Grady was at his desk pouring over business ledgers for the plantation, she approached him.

"You busy?" she asked, standing at the door to the library.

Not having sensed her presence, he turned abruptly. He immediately reacted to her beauty and radiance.

"Ah didn't see you standing there," he apologized as he got to his feet, always the gentleman. "Come in, mah dear."

The flowing skirts of her gown made a rustling noise as she walked across the floor.

"I hope I'm not bothering you," she smiled, giving him a kiss on his cheek.

"Not at all. Ah always have time for the mistress of Hummingbird Hill. And such a beautiful mistress at that. You are the envy of every woman in the county and all the men are envious of me."

She momentarily glanced at the figures in the ledger spread across the desk.

"Are we turning a profit?" she asked.

"Things look good for now," he said, walking to the desk and closing the ledger.

The world of business was no place for a lady.

"Of course it's early in the season. As you know, a lot will depend on the weather, but we seem to be ahead of schedule. Certainly nothing for you to worry your pretty little head about, mah dear."

She smiled, still fascinated by his southern drawl.

"Grady, I was riding today," she began, pretending to be casually interested in the volumes of books on the shelving.

"Wonderful. It was a great day to be out and about. Where did you go?"

"I went up to the bluff where I could look down on the river and the plantation house and the cotton fields."

"You should not have gone alone. If you had told me, I could have sent someone with you."

That was one quality in Grady that did not please her. He always seemed to want to protect her from the things her free spirit chose to pursue.

She dismissed his comment.

"Would Elijah really get in some kind of trouble if he allowed me to ride rather than take the carriage?"

Grady was becoming uneasy with her questioning.

"Whah, no, mah dear," he appeared flustered. "You are the mistress of this plantation and whatever you want to do, you are free to do. And, besides, Elijah knows he should honor your requests."

She walked around the room, glancing occasionally at Grady's appearance. Tall, strong, very virile. His light brown hair was always immaculate even when he'd been out on the plantation all day; and his blue eyes could be both playful and stern.

Her silence bothered him.

"What is it?" he asked. "What seems to be bothering you?"

"Our overseer...Hardy," she said, carefully choosing to use the word *our*. "I saw him in the fields today overseeing the darkies. I guess that's why you employ him...to oversee."

She smiled at her own simplicity.

"Yes?"

"He beat one of the male slaves with his whip."

Her green eyes were flashing as she turned to gaze into his. And for the first time since they had married, she saw something in his that frightened her.

"We've talked about that, Samantha. It's a part of plantation life. It happens sometimes," he defended. "When they are out of line, they must be disciplined."

She merely looked at him, but he seemed to feel as if further explanation should be given.

"Samantha, you've got to stop looking at them as individuals. They are property. We need to have slaves to work the cotton. It is our livelihood. And you profit every day from their labor."

The last was added with a touch of irritation as he flung his arm to accentuate his point by gesturing towards the lavish plantation home with its expensive furnishings.

"I was just asking, my dear. Please don't be upset."

Approaching him, she put her arms around him and looked up at him and smiled.

"I'm going to retire now. Will you be coming soon?"

"Ah will," he relaxed. "Ah just have a little paperwork yet to do. Ah'll be along shortly."

She walked to the huge oak doors and then turned back to him.

"By the way, I do believe the beaten darkie did not do anything to deserve that treatment."

She didn't look back as she exited the room. She had made her point.

He heard the swish of her skirts as she climbed the winding staircase, then made his way to the liquor cabinet and poured himself a drink. Samantha certainly knew how to upset him. As he swallowed the entire amount of liquor in one gulp, he turned as another person entered the room.

"You called, massah?"

"Not tonight, Clover. Not tonight."

Sounds from the Negro cabins floated up to the second floor of the plantation house. Samantha opened her bedroom window to hear the songs that penetrated the night air. Soulful. Mournful, but somehow peaceful and calming.

Izzy was waiting to take the emerald gown Samantha was wearing. The quiet nature of this slender girl was reflected in her large brown eyes. Her beauty was hidden behind the drab dress that hung loosely from her shoulders, appearing to be a couple sizes too big for her. Samantha, however, thought the girl was beautiful with her soft skin the color of burnt sienna and had seen one of the young bucks expressing some interest in her. Although Samantha herself had been a young bride of seventeen, the fourteen year old Izzy was a shy girl, not ready for the harshness of the world, or so Samantha thought. Samantha's instinct was to protect the innocent girl, but she didn't know if that was even possible. Then an overwhelming sadness came over her knowing that Izzy's life would become one of bearing children to *increase the work force.*

"Thank you, Izzy," she said as the slender brown girl took the emerald gown and hung it in the massive closet area.

"Iz you wantin' anythin' more, missus?" Izzy asked humbly.

Noting that Izzy had already brought water for washing and had laid out Samantha's night gown and had turned down the white lace bedspread on the four poster bed, Samantha smiled at the young girl.

"No, thank you, Izzy," she said softly. "That will be all."

Izzy bowed at the waist and backed out the door to the bedroom, closing it behind her.

Of all the slaves on the plantation, Izzy was Samantha's favorite. There was a sweetness about this girl, a gentle spirit. Nothing had been revealed about her parents or her background. Grady said she had been on the plantation for five years and he wasn't sure either of her background. She was quiet and shy and Samantha had many long talks with her and found her to be highly intelligent. She flourished under Samantha's kind treatment and responded by being gracious and kind. Samantha regarded Izzy as more of a companion rather than a slave and had begged Grady to allow her to be Samantha's personal house slave.

Samantha stood staring after her. What Samantha missed most was having a close friend. There were no young ladies *of suitable caliber* as Grady put it nearby to visit with. She recalled the angry discussions she and Grady had over Samantha teaching Izzy to read and write.

"It's just not done," he said. "I am doing these people a favor. I have saved them from life in the pagan jungles. I provide them food and shelter and medicine. In return, they work."

Samantha walked to the window and looked out to the firelight down at the slave cabins and listened to the music floating up from them and wondered where Chase and her family were at this very minute.

3

An Inn Somewhere in Virginia,
Spring 1864

Chase

"One night's lodging, sir," Chase said as he quickly surveyed the room.

The clerk behind the desk peered over his spectacles as he watched Chase sign his name and readily accepted the coin pressed into his hand as he mumbled a weak welcome. One dim light hung over a corner table where several men sat smoking and talking rather loudly. Chase tried to ignore their conversation, but could hear it contained talk about the war. It seemed that was the only topic of conversation these days.

"Room 8 at the top of the stairs and to your right," the clerk said as he removed a key from the box behind him. The scraping noise of the key being slid across the counter grated on Chase's already jagged nerves. Once again he nervously glanced around the room.

"Thank you, my good man," Chase responded. "Where might I find the closest livery?"

Pulling a watch from his vest pocket and checking the time, the small grizzled clerk gestured towards the door.

"Miller's Livery. To the west. Prob'ly fifteen minutes 'til he closes."

"Thanks," Chase said as he headed for the door.

Streets were starting to clear as families hurried home to avoid the perils lurking in the approaching night. Miller's Livery sign was easy to find and Chase hurried in order to get there before the proprietor left for the evening. As he entered the building, his nose filled with the smell of hay and animals. He found the owner just cleaning up.

"Hello," Chase called out.

Chase chose to speak as little as possible for fear he might be viewed as a foreigner. Everyone was suspicious these days. The last thing he needed was his voice giving him away. Clem turned at the sound of the voice, pleased at the prospect of yet another customer here at the end of the day.

"What kin I do fer ya?" he asked.

"A horse. I need a sturdy steed," he replied.

"Got two."

Clem took note of Chase's hat pulled down over his face while he proceeded to make his way to a couple of stalls housing the horses and Chase checked them over before he made his selection.

"How much?"

Clem stroked his beard as if that was a difficult decision to make. He made an offer that included saddle and saddle bags and gear. Chase made a counter offer and Clem accepted the deal.

What Chase needed was a good night's sleep. As he started back to the inn, he realized the tempo of the streets had changed dramatically. No longer were there women and children and families lingering about. All that remained were a few clusters of men. Chase pulled his coat collar up around his face, his hat down over his forehead and moved straight ahead, once again feeling the steel blade against his leg and wishing the gun he carried in his luggage was in a more accessible place. A mist was coming in off the river and there was a chill in the air.

He was within sight of the inn when he realized someone was standing right in his path. He stepped to the side and so did the figure, clearly intending to block Chase's path. As his pulse quickened, he felt the presence of others nearby.

"Suh, express yore preference...union or rebel?"

Chase thought quickly as beads of perspiration broke out across his forehead. Clearing his throat, he hoped his voice would not betray him; and using his best English accent, he forced bravery into his speech.

"Sir, I come from England and I come in peace."

The man's eyes narrowed as he scrutinized Chase's partly hidden face.

"What is your mission, suh?"

"I am headed to South Carolina to visit with my sister who lives there," he offered.

There was a hesitation that seemed to last an eternity. Then apparently satisfied with his answer, the man spoke again.

"Very well, suh. I suggest you make quick work of yore stay. There is much unrest in this country."

"Thank you, sir. I appreciate your advice. Good night."

The man stepped to the side and Chase quickly pressed past them and found Room 8 at the inn. Hours passed by before he fell asleep. Mist from the river was still rolling in when he saddled his horse and started another day of his long journey.

It was past noon when he heard the gun fire. Pulling his horse to a halt, he sat quietly and listened. Not very close, he concluded. Guiding the horse to the west a bit, he carefully chose his path through the underbrush, staying close to the tree line, not willing to expose himself any more than possible to the open fields. It was slower going, but safer in the long run.

He had no idea how many miles he had covered and was feeling grateful to his father for his experience with horseback riding. The tapestry bag had been left that night at the inn and everything had been transferred to saddlebags and a bedroll he had tied on behind him. His gun was tucked inside his jacket, its steely coldness a constant reminder of the danger in his journey. He rode possibly later into the evening than he should have. Shadows crept in early in the seclusion of the trees. Still, he considered that the safest thing to do.

After taking care of the horse and gathering small twigs and dried leaves, he knelt down to build a small fire.

"Don't do it, friend."

The words came out of the dark and Chase wheeled around, reaching for his gun. As his eyes adjusted to the darkness, he saw a slender man probably about his own age standing against a nearby tree. They stared at each other for a few seconds.

"A fire is sure to let the troops know where you are," the stranger offered.

When Chase made no reply, the man continued.

"And it's hard to sort out who's the friend and who's the enemy."

"Thanks," Chase cautiously managed and wondered just who this man was who stood before him...the enemy or the friend.

"You come far?"

Chase hesitated giving out too much information. Instead, he tried to divert the question.

"Far enough," he said. "You?"

"Oh, I've been in this man's war now for over two years."

Chase studied the features of the man, now taking note of his gaunt appearance and ragged clothing...and the rifle that the man leaned against.

"That's a long time."

"Yep."

Finally, Chase pulled some Johnnie cake from his satchel.

"You hungry?" he asked the soldier.

"Hungry?" the man laughed. "There ain't been nothin' but hunger here since this thing started up."

"Come sit down," Chase offered, beginning to feel more comfortable with the situation.

The man put the butt of the rifle out in front of him to take a step and it was then Chase saw the leg...the bloody rag tied around it. The soldier collapsed the minute he started to move. Chase ran to his aid.

"Come on, buddy," he encouraged. "Let's have a look at that leg."

The man groaned with pain as Chase helped him to sit on a fallen log. He ripped the bloody pant leg from the man's injured leg and gasped at the smell. He felt for the man's forehead. Fever for sure. Using what little medical knowledge he had, he cleaned the wound as best as he could and put a fresh bandage on it with fabric he tore from his shirt. That was as much as he could do to make him as comfortable for the night so he settled down close by and finally went off to sleep himself.

When the first rays of sunlight hit his face the following morning, Chase woke with a start; and looking around, he saw the soldier sitting up near a small fire that burned low, saw he was making a noose by weaving some of the vines that grew abundantly on the trees. The stranger had been awake for a while.

"What are you doing?" he asked, rubbing the sleep from his eyes.

"Gotta eat. Don't want to waste the ammunition or call attention to us," the soldier said. "There's a rabbit been playin' around here all mornin' and I aim to get him. Haven't heard any army movement since I woke up. Thought we might venture a fire."

Chase realized this was a good thing. At least his stomach agreed with the proposition. He watched as the soldier carefully outwitted the rabbit, snared it, gutted it and then turned to Chase.

"Now, you go down to the crick and wash him up a bit while I fix somethin' to roast him on."

Chase started to leave and then turned.

"You got a name?"

"Mac," the soldier said. "Short for MacCarthy."

Chase thought for a few moments.

"I was wondering why a soldier is out here by himself."

At first he thought there was no answer forthcoming.

"The leg. Can't keep up. Just left behind."

Again, silence settled over the two men.

Chase wasn't much of an outdoor man, but he was learning from Mac. If rabbit tasted this good, he would learn how to snare them and prepare them himself.

When their stomachs were somewhat satisfied, Chase approached Mac with a proposition. Leaving an injured man behind did not seem quite right to him. He hadn't asked Mac any questions about what part he had played in the war. At this point, Chase was not really concerned with whether Mac was union or rebel. He was merely a man not to be left on his own.

"I don't know where you're headed," he said, "but you're welcome to come along with me."

Mac thought about it a bit.

"Where you goin' ?"

"South. York County, South Carolina. I have a sister there."

Mac was quiet for so long that Chase thought he was refusing his offer.

"Sure," the answer finally came. "I could go along with ya fer a while."

Chase helped him up on the horse and took the reins and walked in front. For the next two days, Chase and Mac walked and talked and Mac told Chase stories of the war and showed him many things along the way about living in the outdoors. By the end of the second day, Chase could judge how close the gun and cannon fire were and had caught a rabbit on his own and learned that moss grows on the north side of trees and wet leaves don't burn that good. He learned how to predict the weather and judge the way the wind was blowing by the smoke of battle. He was even learning the kinds of guns and cannons by their sounds.

But each day Mac grew weaker and the fever was persistent and the leg looked bad. The third day there was not much talking and Chase had to stop frequently because Mac was in so much pain. When Chase woke up the fourth day, he found this was one battle Mac had lost.

As Chase dug as deep as he could and placed the body in the hallowed out spot and covered it with as many rocks as he could find, he took time to carve a piece of wood with the word *Mac* on it. Although he had an urgency to find Samantha, it was the least he could do. He kept Mac's knife and rifle and ammunition, partly as a souvenir of their short friendship and partly because Chase was aware of how important they could be to survival. And Mac's shoes were invaluable so he tied the laces together and threw them over his shoulder. Chase appreciated Mac's friendship and little did he know that those things Mac had taught him would become so valuable on his way to Samantha and Hummingbird Hill.

June 8, 1864 Washington, D. C.

The atmosphere was grim in the Stewart library. Edward and Clinton Stewart sat in the bulky wooden chairs facing their father's massive oak desk and his somber demeanor. Sylvester Stewart peered over his glasses at his two older sons.

"Lincoln's been nominated for re-election," he stated. "I fear there is much unrest in the country over this election. The war has gone on longer than anticipated and people are edgy at best. What have you heard?"

Edward was the first to speak.

"Lincoln has a lot of support, but there is a lot of opposition as well. I fear for any man trying to lead this country through this hell."

"Unrest in the cabinet itself," Clinton added. "Division over all that's happened."

"And the fighting?"

"According to the reports coming in, things are bad everywhere. Fighting all through the south. Mississippi, Louisiana, Georgia, Virginia. All taking big hits. Lee stalled Grant's drive toward Richmond in May, but I don't know how long the confederacy can last. And it hasn't been as easy as the union commanders first thought."

"Umm," Sylvester Stewart nodded his head.

"I think the confederacy has held on to the Red River area in Louisiana," Clinton offered. "I thought things might have changed when Grant assumed command back in March. Now I don't know."

"What about supplies?"

This directed at Edward.

"We've been busy, but I fear we are falling short of the demand. Who would have thought this insanity would still be going on? Right now, I'm saying we're doing the best we can. I have people working day and night in an effort to get supplies through the confederate lines. Still, I think we're in better shape than the confederacy."

"On the positive side, I hear some of the union prisoners who escaped from Libby Prison in Richmond made it," Clinton mused.

"And the Hunley took down the Houstonic. A submarine, of all things. If the confederates are smart enough to build a submarine and sink a ship, they could out maneuver the north in this war."

"But are they organized enough to do such a thing? Do they have the resources? Right now it looks like each side is giving as good as they get."

"Yes, just one bloody battle after another. And it seems as if neither side is making progress."

"Washington has become a mecca for refugees. Our churches have been converted to hospitals. People are living in squalor. Not enough food here let alone to be sent to the troops. But it has become my job to find supplies and find ways of transporting them."

"I know you're working day and night, Edward. I fear for those we know. Has anything been heard from Nathan Clevinger since he left?"

"His parents had two letters early on. Nothing for months now."

"And Chase?"

"Nothing since he left the state of Virginia. Maybe I shouldn't have sent him. Perhaps it was too much to ask. Maybe my judgement was clouded."

"I take it that no one has heard from Samantha either?"

Sylvester shook his head sadly.

"Your mother does not need to know the specifics."

And with that remark, tears formed in his eyes.

"One thing I know about my little brother," Edward stated. "He is not a quitter; and if anyone could get through, it would be Chase. You know, he and Nathan and Samantha have always had this sort of connection between them. I am willing to bet that somehow that will keep all three of them going."

"I pray daily for his safety," Clinton added.

"None of this should reach your mother's ears," Sylvester said with finality.

The fire in the fireplace that warded off the early June chill crackled as silence descended on the Stewart men. Clinton and Edward saw the grimness in their father's face as the firelight played across it.

4

Four Years Earlier
Hummingbird Hill, South Carolina,
April, 1860

Samantha

More than a dozen Negro children sat under a live oak tree on a Sunday morning as they listened to Samantha Reynolds tell the story of David and Goliath. Their eyes were wide with her descriptive narrative and Samantha told the details with a flair for the dramatic. However, that was no different than when she had shared the stories of the baby Moses hidden in a woven basket of reeds on the Nile River or the story of Daniel in the lion's den or the parting of the Red Sea so the children of Israel could cross on dry land.

"And David was able to slew the giant with a stone from his sling shot," she explained as she showed the children a simple version of a sling shot, secretly thanking Chase and Nathan for her expertise in executing the weapon.

But the Sunday Bible session was interrupted by the arrival of the master of the plantation.

"Samantha," Grady roared. "Have I not made my wishes clear?"

Samantha whirled around, not having been aware of his approach. She saw the evil in Grady's eyes and terror struck at her heart. Turning towards her audience of little ones, she quickly recovered enough to dismiss them.

"That will be the end of our story for today," she said kindly. "I will have a new story for you next Sunday."

The children quickly scampered away, glad to be away from Massah Grady.

Grady was livid.

"Next Sunday? Really, Samantha, if ah have anything to say about it, there will be no next Sunday or any other day," he fumed.

"How can a man who claims to be Christian deny the word of God to these children? Am I correct that the good word does command to go to all people?"

Her intelligence and her calmness always unnerved him.

"What is it you are attempting to do, Samantha? Ah forbid you to do this. Ya'all have pushed mah patience beyond reason. Must ah summon Hardy to give you a lesson? Or would you rather ah do it mahself?"

Samantha's eyes grew wide in terror.

"Sir, I would suggest to you that would not be in your best interest."

Grady muttered as he strode back to his horse and vaulted into the saddle and raced off.

Samantha stood looking after him, her pulse beating rapidly, her heart breaking within her. How had the man she married disappeared right before her eyes?

It was to be the party of the year. A perfect warm spring evening in the upcountry with the rich smell of magnolias penetrating the air and gentle breezes floating over the Catawba. The plantation house never looked more elegant. Under Samantha's careful eye and with Clover's hard work, every corner of Hummingbird Hill had been scrubbed and polished. Callie had prepared the most elegant choices of desserts, even some delights from northern kitchens at Samantha insistence. Punch bowls were filled and every piece of glass sparkled. Huge bouquets of the most beautiful early spring flowers from the bountiful gardens adorned tables throughout the hall and formal area. Wooden tables had been so highly polished, the bouquets were reflected in them. Samantha had begged and Grady had finally given in to hiring a small group that would be playing music for listening or dancing.

Ladies arriving in handsome buggies pulled by spirited horses displayed the finest dresses in the most gorgeous array of colors and fabrics, complete with capes and bonnets to match. Samantha's Negro house slaves, moving silently through the rooms, carefully took wraps as the guests arrived. Some of the husbands rode in the carriages with their wives and some chose to accompany them on horseback.

Grady met their guests at the front door and escorted them into the parlor.

Samantha made her entrance, stopping at the top of the grand staircase, pausing to drink in the scene; or perhaps she was letting her guests drink in her beauty. Her dark hair was pulled back and threaded with coral colored ribbon, ribbons that matched the silky coral gown that molded around her torso and waist and then spread gracefully to the floor. Coral ribbon at her neck highlighted a creamy cameo which matched the cream colored lace that trimmed her dress. Tiny cameos at her ears matched the one at her neck and shone with stark beauty against her dark curls. As she descended the winding staircase into the front hall, it was almost as if the entire group of guests were held spellbound at the foot of the stairs.

Colonel Pearce was the first to speak.

"Grady Reynolds!" he exclaimed. "How on earth did you ever get so lucky?"

Then he moved to take Samantha's hand as she neared the bottom of the staircase. She greeted her guests with the cordial manner for which she had become known. Men jostled for position to kiss the back of her hand and whisper sweet words. Women graciously found something to compliment.

As the evening wore on, Samantha became bored with the polite conversation from the southern wives of Grady's guests. There was only so much to be said about plantation life and the *finer things of life* as Grady so graciously put it. Although Samantha's female guests were assembled in the parlor, Samantha struggled to keep an eye on the library where the male guests were assembled. She overheard only snippets of their conversation, but she thought it much more interesting than which woman had been invited to some party in Charleston or what the latest trend in fashion was. And she could care less that Colonel and Mrs. Pearce were sending their daughter abroad for an education.

Sounds of conversation drifted in from the library, calling Samantha to listen, blocking the idle conversation she shared with the women.

"Grady, it's going to happen whether we want it or not. It's inevitable."

"Ya'all are probably right, Jed. These rumors have been going on now for months. And what's more, unrest is on the increase."

"England will get involved if their supply of cotton is withheld. You can bet on that. It's a matter of economics. They'll have to get involved. They'll have no choice."

"Ah don't know, Colonel, Ah've heard they may not want to get involved."

"The northern textile mills can't operate without our supply of cotton. Cotton is just too important. They'll fall in a matter of months."

"But are we organized enough to enter into something more?"

"Emotion is running high. Support is growing."

"We're too far away from Richmond and Charleston to do much good."

"All ah know is that York County in the great state of South Carolina will rise to the cause and organize troops."

"You're convinced it will be all out war then?"

"No doubt in mah mind about it. Yankees need to be put in their place. They don't know how things are done here in the south."

Right in the middle of Mrs. Chaucer telling about her picturesque gardens, Samantha excused herself and moved to the library.

Knowing the topic of conversation was unrest in the south over slavery and the cotton industry, Samantha felt the need to be informed. Isn't that what Papa had taught her? *You can't ever have too much information,* he had often told her. And besides, she found it tremendously interesting.

As five southern ladies sat in astonishment, Samantha made her way into the library and placed her hand in Grady's arm. All conversation seemed to cease at her entrance and she became the focal point.

"Excuse me, gentlemen," she said sweetly. "Please don't stop your conversation because of me."

They stood there in their best finery for the occasion, looking elegant and smug, each with his own selection of liquor in his hand.

Grady was the first to speak.

"I'm sorry to disappoint you, mah dear," he said, "but nothing said in this room would be of any interest to you."

He laughed uncomfortably, unsure of what his wife of less than two years would do or say.

"Are you quite sure?" she smiled, disregarding his look of dismay. "I come from a household of men and I've always found their conversations quite stimulating."

"Really?" Colonel Pearce entered the conversation. "Tell us about your family, Samantha."

"Oh, that's alright, Colonel," Grady interrupted. "Samantha has female guests to entertain."

Samantha dismissed his proposition.

"I don't mind, Grady, dear. Colonel, I am of the northern persuasion."

She let her words sink in before she continued.

"I have a father and mother and three brothers; so you see, I am quite used to men and their ideas. Although I will say, a southern gentleman's ideas are probably a bit different than those I've grown used to."

Her words were smooth and soft but carried a deadly harshness.

"What is your family's business?" Mr. Prescott interjected.

"Oh, law," she smiled innocently. "Just boring law. And a little politics. My oldest brother is in the firm with father. My middle brother is in the import-export business."

She pretended she did not notice the raised eyebrows that statement caused.

"And your other brother, my dear?"

"Just a fun-loving soul like myself. I dare say we got into our share of mischief as children."

There was a ripple of laughter among the men and then Colonel Pearce spoke again.

"I dare say, Samantha, you probably can still get into your share of mischief."

He gave her a sharp wink of his eye as his handle bar mustache twitched.

Another round of laughter.

Grady was embarrassed by her behavior. Samantha ignored his attitude.

"Grady, dear," she said, turning towards him. "Let's take advantage of this wonderful music you've provided. Gentlemen, please feel free to ask your wives to dance."

With a nod to the musicians, she took Grady's arm and proceeded to dance and they were soon joined by the other guests. She pretended not to feel the stiffness in his body. Grady Reynolds was clearly upset by his young wife's behavior.

Colonel Pearce, twirling Miranda Pearce around the room, kept his eyes on their young hostess.

"Samantha Reynolds is surely a breath of fresh air, isn't she?"

"I really hadn't noticed," Mrs. Pearce replied.

As Jed Prescott attempted to dance with his wife and tried to avoid stepping on her toes, he commented.

"Mrs. Reynolds is ravishing, isn't she?"

"Oh, really?" Mrs. Prescott answered.

Later that evening as Samantha sat before the mirror in her bedroom brushing her hair, Grady bolted through the door. His face was red with anger.

"Hello, dear," Samantha greeted, ignoring his mood.

Although Samantha had been surprised when she arrived at Hummingbird Hill to find her bedroom was separate from that of the master of the house, she thought perhaps it was a southern tradition.

After all, when Grady was in need of company, he freely came and went.

"There are some things we need to make clear," he said, standing behind her looking at their reflection in the mirror.

Stopping from brushing our her hair, she looked at him in the mirror, not failing to notice his angry red face.

"Yes?" she said and once again continued brushing.

"Your behavior tonight was totally unacceptable."

His words caused both anger and disappointment to rise within her, but she had learned early in their relationship to control her feelings.

"What's on your mind, Grady?" she asked as she got up from the bench and faced him.

She was beautiful and just as enticing as she had been when he brought her to Hummingbird Hill. He had known about her spirit, but he thought he could mold her into a southern belle. He hadn't counted on her being quite as smart as she had turned out to be. It was something he admired, but also something that made him uneasy.

"Tonight," he stammered. "No self-respecting woman... plantation owner's wife... would have come into a group of men and entered into conversation. Yore place is to entertain mah guests' wives and talk about...about...about women things. Leave the business to the men. That's the way it's done here in the south."

She remained calm.

"So, let me get the full impact of what you are saying," she began. "You want me to be dull and boring like all the other women I've met? You do not wish me to have a thought in my head. Indeed, are you afraid of what I might think or know?"

"It's not that," his anger was growing. "It's about how things are done here, about what is expected of you."

"Have I not fulfilled my duties as lady of the manor? I thought I did a good job of entertaining your guests."

Now she was goading him.

"Women have their place."

She pulled back the cover on the bed and slipped out of her robe.

"I am not one of your slaves, Grady," she said as she sat on the edge of the bed. "I will not submit to a bunch of silly rules made up by a bunch of stuffy, stodgy men who keep their women ignorant. Now I'm going to bed. Good night."

He clenched his fists and stomped from the room.

Once he had gone, she lay there finally able to breathe again. She would not let Grady know how upset she really was. After hearing the downstairs doors close behind him, she got to her feet and watched him walk across the clearing to the slave cabins.

Father had taught his only daughter to be independent and to think for herself. Although she was protected by three older brothers, she was also encouraged to think and reason. Would these very things cause her to lose a husband?

5

———————— ⌒◟∾◞⌒ ————————

*Virginia Countryside
1864*

Chase

Chase woke to the sound of marching. Grabbing his gear, kicking dirt over the remaining warm ashes of his fire and leading his horse behind a grove of small trees, he listened carefully and held his breath. He reached for the gun tucked in his belt. Union troops or southern? At this point it didn't make much difference. He just wanted to avoid either side.

Sounds grew fainter as minutes passed and he perceived the troops had continued on their way and once again his presence had gone undetected. His lungs filled with air as he began to breathe normally again. Quickly organizing his belongings, he mounted the horse and started at a slow pace, weaving his way through the trees. If his sense of direction was still intact, he was well away from the battles on the eastern part of the state where most of the fighting was taking place. Not that skirmishes weren't ongoing all over the state. From all reports he'd heard, no area would be secure; but less fighting would probably be taking place to the west. And what difference did that make? Any battle that took lives...and what battle didn't...you could be just as dead either way if you happened to be in the wrong place at the right time.

Maybe he should have gone against his father's wishes and enlisted anyway. That's what Nate had done. Enlisted right away but only a couple of letters from him had arrived. It had been an emotional good-bye. First Samantha getting married and moving and then Nate going off to the war. Breaking up the threesome was painful. What good times the three of them had as children...Chase, Nate and Samantha. Not only as children, but right through the teenage years until Amanda broke the trio apart. The three were inseparable, getting into scrapes and situations. And hadn't they laughed and enjoyed themselves? He was pretty sure Nate had a thing for Samantha; and he would have sworn Samantha was sweet on Nate, too, but then Grady came along and swept her off her feet. Chase always regretted that in a way. Maybe now even more. If Samantha and Nate had married, Chase wouldn't be trudging through these trees, these streams, these rocky hills and meadows, wondering if a gun would be pointed at his head at any minute.

He shuddered to think that even if Samantha and Nate had married and Nate had gone off to war, he could possibly be consoling a widow as well. Well, he hoped he would never have to face that. In a perfect world, he would find and bring Samantha back to Washington to their ailing mother and Nate would return from the battlefield unharmed.

Anyway, the two boys had continued their fun, but somehow it wasn't the same without Samantha. Nate had attended the wedding, disappeared during the after party and had been really quiet ever since. Even the advances of Sarah Melissa Colter hadn't brought him out of his slump. And if anyone could do that, she certainly was up to the task. Sarah Melissa Colter was the biggest flirt Washington had ever seen and had been directly responsible for improving the outlook of many men in the area, including some of those who served in government capacities.

Chase wondered where Nate was now and if he was safe in this bloody war. But Samantha was his first priority. Finding her and taking her back to Washington was his mission; and if that meant inconvenience to him, he would deal with it. Right now he needed to put more miles between him and the regiment that had just passed by.

All went well until about two o'clock in the afternoon when he had to leave the seclusion of the tree line and cross a small meadow. He was almost half way across the open space when he had the peculiar sensation that things were just too quiet. Suddenly a shot rang out, breaking the silence. Fortunately for him, he had been comfortably out of range and the marksman fired too soon, thus missing his target. Chase kicked his horse into a gallop; and leaning close down against the horse's neck, he headed straight for the seclusion of the next grove of trees. For a brief second, he wondered if that was a smart move. Perhaps he should have just retreated back to the grove he just left. Too late. His only choice now was to move straight ahead as fast as he could push the horse. He was just about to think he would make the cover of the trees when another shot came straight at him. There was more than one attacker and he was riding right into danger. Pulling his horse up short, he turned direction and galloped farther to his right. That proved to be the best choice since the gunfire now appeared to be coming from behind him.

When he was comfortable that he had made the right decision and was not being followed and had reached the seclusion of the trees, he slowed the horse to a walk; and it was only then that he felt the sharp sting in his shoulder. Looking down, he saw blood oozing from his shirt. Well, it would just have to wait. First priority had to be knowing he was securely a safe distance away from the gunfire. He traveled on until the sun was beginning to wane and only then did he stop to examine the wound. Superficial. But if there was one thing he had learned from Mac, it was that no wound should go untreated. He found a stream and washed it thoroughly and used some of the precious whisky he carried in his flask to treat it.

Questioning the wisdom of building a fire, he merely wrapped his blanket around him and tried to sleep. No matter which way he laid, the shoulder burned and throbbed. Finally he slept fitfully until dawn and then decided he might just as well push forward. He was tired from his night's unrest and tired from long days of traveling so perhaps he wasn't as vigilant as he should have been. He hadn't been aware of the fact he was being followed until it was too late. He only knew that he was grabbed from behind and then hit the ground with a thud, finding himself in a struggle with a man, an animal? At first he wasn't quite sure. It turned out to be a man.

Chase had been in some scraps before, not life or death ones; but defending oneself was a matter of instinct. When he finally broke the stranger's hold, he saw that his opponent was a young soldier about his own age. He ran at him; and hitting him square in the stomach, the two sprawled on the ground. The man gained the upper hand and ended up on top of him and proceeded to pound Chase in the face. Chase temporarily put aside the pain in his shoulder; and placing both hands against the man's shoulders, he attempted to loosen his hold. Pushing him back with sheer strength, he was able to bring his knees up and kick. The man fell backwards and Chase wasted no time in pouncing on him. Pain in his knuckles did not prevent him from punching over and over again until he was sure he had overpowered him.

Even though he felt the crunch of the man's jaw against his fist, he was unrelenting. Every time the man made it to his feet, Chase knew he had no choice but to knock his adversary down again. His vision blurred with blood oozing from a gash above his eye and he staggered with exhaustion. Finally the man groaned and lay still.

Chase checked briefly to see if he was still alive; and believing that was true, he found his horse, mounted and flew once more to put as many miles as he could behind him.

His shoulder ached, the gash over his eye stung and his knuckles were raw. He would go a little farther before he would find a safe place to stop. Safe place? How ridiculous was that concept? For tonight, safe turned out to be a deserted barn. It was falling down but it was dry and there was a bit of hay to cushion his aching body and he found a small amount of oats which the horse relished. Chase slept until the sun was well up into the sky.

6

Hummingbird Hill,
Early Spring 1861

Samantha

"But I want to do something special for her," Samantha pouted.

"Samantha, it's just not done! How can Ah convince you that these slaves are property?"

"But Izzy has been very good to me. And that's the least I can do to repay her."

Samantha was persistent, a quality which irritated Grady beyond control.

"Repay? Repay?" he yelled. "It's her obligation. You've already gone against my wishes by teaching her to read and write. Educated slaves will only mean trouble. If you start being kind to them, they will think they have rights, deserve more than ah am willing to give. Ah already give them a home and take care of their needs. They have a better life because of me."

But Samantha was firm and her dainty foot tapped impatiently and her arms were firmly planted across her chest. Grady knew he was losing the battle.

"Grady, there is no room for discussion. I've made up my mind."

Over the last several months, Grady had learned that Samantha indeed was strong willed. He was finding out that it was probably best to ignore what he had been unable to change. Still, she was a beautiful woman, managed the household well and every one of his associates commented on her attractiveness and intelligence. But she was not the submissive wife he had thought she would be and resentment towards her was increasing. And isn't that what a good plantation wife did? Be submissive? Leave business to the men? However, her relationship with the slave population was his biggest concern. She just seemed to not understand the importance of slavery to the cotton industry. Well, that's what he got for marrying a northerner with northern ideas.

More important on the horizon was the news that Colonel Pearce had brought last evening. Growing unrest in the south along with rumors that South Carolina was preparing to secede from the union were of more immediate concern. Troops were being rallied across the state at this very minute for an all-out war. And somehow he had to tell Samantha that he would be joining the cause. He could just hear her reaction to that!

Maybe that was for the best. He was finding her less and less appealing and a hatred was growing within him.

Right now he had plantation book work to finish and he needed to focus on something besides Samantha. Turning towards his desk, he took a key from his vest pocket and unlocked the top drawer. Carefully removing the ledger, he turned the pages until he found the page he was looking for...the page that listed the names of the female slaves. His finger slid down the page of names, each line containing the name of a female slave, an age, a date and then followed the line across to a second date plus the word either *male* or *female* and then another name. Clover's name was in the list five different times. Four sons...Samuel, Isaiah, Esau, Adam. That was good. The fifth entry had not yet been filled in with a child's name. Further down the list was Izzy's name. Age fourteen years.

It was time.

Samantha found the perfect piece of fabric. Izzy would indeed have a new dress for her upcoming wedding. Seeing the love in Izzy and Johns' eyes left no doubt in Samantha's mind that they would be good for each other. Samantha had no idea of what she might be starting with the slaves. Repercussions to her decisions were the furthest things from Samantha's mind. She only knew she wanted to reward this perfect little girl for her sweet ways. And the look in Izzy's eyes as Samantha fit the dress to her was reward enough. The light blue dress sprinkled with darker blue flowers would be ready in plenty of time for Izzy's marriage to John which was still two weeks away.

It was a balmy morning as Samantha would remember later, (March 20th, 1862). A fog had settled in from the river and had not yet dissipated. Samantha was walking through the garden when she saw Izzy coming towards the plantation house from the cabins. The dress was ready for another fitting and Samantha was excited about it.

"Izzy, come on up to the house," Samantha called. "I've almost finished the dress and I'd like for you to try it on."

Samantha could tell from the manner in which Izzy walked that something was wrong...desperately wrong. Izzy staggered and almost fell to the ground. Samantha came to her rescue, steadying the girl with her arms and helping her walk to the house. As they passed through the kitchen, Callie and the other Negro women working there fell silent, stopping their chores of peeling and stirring and frying and baking. Smells of ham and biscuits and fried potatoes from breakfast still hung in the air. Ignoring the look on their faces, Samantha hurried to help Izzy up the stairs and was painfully aware that it was all Izzy could do to make her body climb the steps.

Not until they were in the confines of Samantha's bedroom did she feel the full impact of Izzy's injuries. Eyes red from crying, bruises, cuts, swollen lips. Most daunting of all was the look in Izzy's eyes. Something had torn the joy from Izzy's beautifully innocent brown eyes.

"Izzy, what is it? What has happened to you?" Samantha said as she helped the girl into a chair, noticing the wincing in pain as she did so.

"Nothin', missus," the girl whispered with trembling lips as yet more tears slipped down her cheeks and dropped down on her faded gray dress. She reached up to brush them with the back of her hand.

"This is more than nothing," Samantha said, showing her concern as she poured water from the porcelain pitcher to the bowl. Taking a fresh cloth, she proceeded to wipe the tears and cuts as gently as possible.

After more unanswered questions, Samantha was quite sure she would not get any response, so she told Izzy she would not ask her to work that day. And it certainly wasn't a good day to bring up the blue dress.

"You need some time off," Samantha proposed.

"Oh, but ah haz to work, missus," she stammered, clearly having a better concept of the consequences than Samantha had.

"No, you don't," Samantha defended in a soft voice.

"But massah…"

Izzy's lips began to quiver again as she broke into tears once more.

"Hush, now," Samantha consoled. "Let *me* take care of Mr. Reynolds."

Izzy flinched at his name and Samantha saw the terror that came in the little girl's eyes. Samantha walked her back downstairs and out the back door.

"Spend some time in the garden," she said as she patted the girl on the shoulder. "Then you can help Callie in the kitchen the rest of the day."

Callie had a motherly way of making everything better.

Izzy had never before exhibited any fear of being touched, but she drew back.

Samantha returned to the plantation house by way of the back door. As she did, she heard some talk over the clanging of the pots and pans among the women in the kitchen. Samantha stopped at the steps to the kitchen and listened to the conversation. As she did, a sickening feeling swept across her body.

"It was her first time," one woman said. "The first time is always the worst."

"Do you think Ms. Samantha know?" came another voice.

"She don't know how things iz."

"Hush, now, we'll all be in trouble if they hear us talkin' 'bout sech things."

Samantha recognized that wise voice as belonging to Callie. She quickly exited the back porch, hoping the women indeed did not know she was anywhere around. Walking quickly to the stables, she asked Elijah to saddle her horse. Samantha needed to get away and think.

Somehow riding like the wind did not keep the ache in Samantha's body from seizing hold of her insides or keep the tears from stinging her eyes. There were so many questions concerning the slaves that were left unanswered...things she could not comprehend. If only she could talk with Chase or Nathan. Nathan! How she longed to look into his twinkling eyes once more...the same expression he wore when he was teasing or tormenting her. They had been so happy...the three of them...Chase, Samantha and Nathan. But this was no longer about three young people and their escapades of youth. This was about real life.

Were her suspicions about her husband true? The fear that gripped her heart told her they probably were. But she needed proof. Isn't that what father always told her? Indisputable proof. How many times had he preached the things she should know? Suspicion substantiated by proof and then reasonable conclusions could be drawn. Well, the first was already realized. Samantha certainly had her suspicions about how business was conducted at Hummingbird Hill. And she wasn't at all sure she was pleased about what she suspected.

Sounds of buggy tires crunched against the path that led to the Prescott plantation. The Prescotts were the closest thing to neighbors the Reynolds had. Samantha could see the back of Elijah's head before her and wished she could sit beside him on the buggy seat and talk with him throughout the journey. But even Samantha knew that would be inappropriate behavior for a southern lady. Besides, her questions and his answers would only put Elijah in danger.

Samantha settled back in the seat of the buggy and watched as the beautiful scenery of South Carolina passed by. Yes, Grady had been right about that…this part of the southland was exquisite.

The Prescott plantation was smaller than Hummingbird Hill, but it was still elegant and Samantha observed the familiar plantation life being carried out with darkies working in the fields and lazy morning chores being accomplished.

Elijah pulled the buggy to a halt in front of the house, dismounted from the high bench seat and came around the side of the buggy to put a step on the ground so Samantha could exit the carriage. Afterwards, he would continue to the stable where the horse would rest and perhaps Elijah would be able to talk with his friend, Seth, until Mrs. Reynolds was ready to leave again. Having seen the carriage coming up the front lawn, Nancy Prescott opened the front door and hurried down the steps to welcome her guest.

"Samantha, mah dear, how nice to see you. What brings you our way this fine mornin'?"

Nancy Prescott was just about the closest neighbor to Hummingbird Hill even though it was still a significant ride. But Samantha needed to make this fact finding mission. However, she thought it wise to take the buggy this time and allowed Elijah to drive her rather than come by horseback.

"Just a good day for visiting," Samantha answered, clearly avoiding her reason for the visit.

"Well, do come up on the veranda," Mrs. Prescott invited. "There's such a nice breeze today."

Samantha followed Nancy Prescott to the veranda and settled into one of the oversized rocking chairs while Nancy gave orders for fresh lemonade and tea cakes to be served. Samantha observed the Negro children playing near the cabins, unsupervised while their parents worked nearby. The Prescotts had only a few slaves compared to those Grady owned. There were two Prescott sons to share in the future of the Prescott plantation…sixteen year old Luke Prescott and his fourteen year old brother, Joshua.

When Samantha married Grady, she had considered the possibilities of becoming a mother, but it hadn't happened. A curse or a blessing? In light of her suspicions, she wasn't sure.

Samantha's thoughts were interrupted by the arrival of lemonade and tea cakes.

Using her best social demeanor, Samantha accepted the southern hospitality, all the while wanting to get to her real reason for being there.

"Nancy, these are absolutely delicious," she exclaimed with perfect southern manners.

"Yes," Nancy Prescott answered, "our Delilah has been with the family for quite some time and makes the best southern fried chicken and cornbread in South Carolina!"

She rethought her statement.

"Of course, your Callie is one of the finest cooks as well."

Small talk and polite conversation were not Samantha's strong points.

"Nancy, how does Jed treat the darkies?"

Nancy Prescott drew in a deep breath.

"Oh, I imagine our darkies are treated just about like others in the south," she defended.

Sensing no real animosity, Samantha continued.

"Are they treated kindly?"

"Well, they *are* property, mah dear. Ah can see ya'all are struggling with somethin'. And ah think ah can understand your concern. It's your northern upbringin'. Ah was raised in the south so ah understand the situation. If we did not have slaves, we would not be able to bring in the cotton crop. And cotton is a very important part of our way of life. It's a matter of economics."

"Does Jed visit the female slaves?"

There is was…as blunt as it could be asked. Nancy Prescott's body tensed for a few seconds and then relaxed.

"It's what they do," she said softly, reaching over to touch Samantha's hand. "It is a way to increase the colony, you know. Every slave child born on a plantation becomes the property of the plantation owner."

She sat back in her chair and began to rock, as she sipped the tart lemonade.

"Besides, it helps fulfill a man's needs, you understand. Makes things easier on we women sometimes."

How could this woman be so accepting of the situation? Although Samantha recoiled at the statement of the facts, she had more questions to ask.

"Do they keep records?"

"Oh, my, yes. Although I've never actually seen them. It's really not a lady's business."

Samantha winced at the same things she had heard from Grady. Were all southern women brainwashed? But she pressed forward with her questions.

"Does he ever have one woman in particular that he finds pleasure in?"

Mrs. Prescott fidgeted with the skirt of her dress.

Had Samantha's questions hit a nerve?

"Ah suppose it's possible," she answered, "but not very likely. Please understand such behavior does not mean he does not care for you, mah dear. It's nothing personal. It's just a way of life, Samantha. Learn to accept it."

Even as Nancy Prescott heard her own words being said from her own mouth, she was quite sure this young woman from the north in no way would be accepting her advice.

Samantha was just a bit concerned as she saw Jed Prescott's horse coming up the lane to Hummingbird Hill at a full gallop. Surely her visit with Nancy Prescott would not warrant a visit from him.

"Grady," Samantha called, "Jed Prescott is coming up the lane and he seems to be in a terrible hurry."

Grady came to the veranda from the library.

"Why do you think he's in such a hurry, Grady?"

48

They didn't have long to wait to find out. Jed slid from his horse almost before the horse had come to a halt.

"It's happened, Grady," he shouted. "We've attacked Fort Sumter. South Carolina has seceded."

Grady turned to Samantha.

"Go inside, Samantha. This is business for men."

Samantha gave him a look he ignored as he hurried down the front steps where he and Jed talked in soft tones.

Retreating to the front hallway, Samantha took refuge in one corner and kept the front door open just a bit, hoping to hear what was being said. The most information she could ascertain was that South Carolina was rallying troops to aid in what had become a full-fledged war.

As she secretly listened, she turned to stare into the eyes of Clover who was just finishing polishing Grady's desk in the library. For an instant, their eyes met and the two women exchanged a mutual dislike. No doubt Clover would report Samantha's behavior to Grady. Then Clover disappeared down the hallway, waddling just a bit with the added weight of her pregnancy.

"Ah don't know how this will all turn out," Grady ranted. "But South Carolina has led the way," he said with pride. "The cotton industry needs to be preserved; and if slaves are set free, there will be no more industry. I know other states will follow. We will persevere! We will lead."

Never had she seen such passion in him as he paced back and forth in the library with the excitement and enthusiasm of a mad man. She wondered if Grady was even aware she was standing in the same room with him. Sometimes the man she married was so far hidden she didn't even recognize him. She stood quietly listening to the man she no longer understood.

"Prescott says troops are being formed right now and Ah plan to go down to Richmond with Prescott and lend my support."

Changes this news would bring in her life were still obscure; yet she sensed the impact would be great.

"How soon will you be leaving?" she asked calmly.

"Possibly in a day or two."

Although the news took her somewhat by surprise, she appeared to remain calm on the outside.

"Do you plan to be gone long?"

He was clearly agitated by her question.

"I don't know, Samantha. How do I know how long this confrontation will last? We will do everything it takes to preserve the south. But I need to take care of some things here first…to make sure things run smoothly while I'm gone," he added.

She thought before she spoke, but she spoke with confidence.

"Perhaps if you shared the business of the plantation with me, I would be able to carry on in your absence."

She said it calmly and softly, but the impact it carried was heavy. He whirled and glared at her with hatred in his eyes.

"You really think a Yankee can run a plantation?"

Of interest to her was the fact that he had not focused on the fact she was a woman or lacked intelligence, but the fact that she had been born in a different part of the country.

"I'm quite sure *this Yankee* could get the job done," she smiled.

"Hardy will stay here. He will oversee the darkies and the crops. You'd probably give all of them their freedom if you were in charge," he snapped. "You being the tender hearted woman you are."

"Very well, my dear," she said as she turned, "whatever pleases you."

———

The next few days were hectic with Grady getting things in order to leave. There would be an entire troop from York County, consisting of men and boys from every corner of the county under the command of Colonel Pearce. Jed Prescott would be volunteering as well as his older son, Luke. Grady spent a great deal of time in deep conversation with Colonel Pearce discussing strategy and plans. Weapons were checked and double checked and Samantha was relieved when she saw a set of pistols and a rifle and a hand gun still in their places. Not that she expected trouble, but she felt more comfortable knowing they were there.

It was quite by accident that she happened to be passing by his room as Grady removed a key from his vest pocket and placed it in a small wooden box on his chest of drawers. He was unaware of her presence and she discreetly continued down the hallway, tucking that bit of information in her head for future use.

If Samantha felt anything, it was that she was perhaps being neglected, overlooked, ignored, told she was unimportant. Seeing Grady's zest for battle was both overwhelming and disturbing.

"Have you seen Mr. Grady?" Samantha asked of Callie.

Callie was a large woman, not tall, but round. There was a motherly quality about her. Besides being a good cook, she was a good manager of the kitchen, gently encouraging those who worked with her to put forth good effort. On occasion, Samantha had even seen Callie react to Clover's attitude, but never once saw the two have words. Kindness and empathy were just a natural part of Callie's personality.

"No, 'um," Callie answered, her strong hands working in a pan of dough. "Callie ain't seen the massah since early mornin'."

But Callie's huge brown eyes gave her away as they turned in the direction of the barn. Whether it was intentional or not, it conveyed a message. Samantha picked up her skirts and started to cross the yard towards the barn. But she stopped short as Grady emerged from the barn, fastening his jacket with one hand and brushing back his brown hair with the other. Samantha stopped in midstride. Grady pushed past her without a word, ignoring the questions in her eyes.

But Samantha's attention was drawn back to the squeaking barn door. A disheveled Clover stood in the doorway, her blouse unbuttoned to reveal her curves, a piece of straw caught in her hair. Her eyes were still mean, but there was another emotion in them now.

Humiliated, Samantha hurried back to the house.

Another woman may have handled the situation differently; but Samantha, fueled by what she had just witnessed, confronted him that evening in the library.

"I have some questions," she started.

"I'm really busy," he answered, not bothering to look up from his ledgers, not willing to deal with any more issues with her.

"It's about Clover."

"She giving you trouble again?" he said, still engrossed in his work. "We've had this conversation before, Samantha. Don't let her get to you. She's a good worker. And has provided us with four male children."

"About that…" she said, cautiously.

There was something in her voice that caused him to turn to look at her.

"Is this something that is a concern of yours?" he flashed.

Her passion for the subject did not go unnoticed.

"Samantha, leave well enough alone," he demanded.

"I can't, Grady. I find the practice detestable and what you did to Izzy…"

Jumping to his feet, he towered above her.

"Now that really *is* none of your business!"

Her green eyes were filled with hurt and anger; his eyes were haughty and arrogant.

"You have spoiled that girl with your pampering and ideas about education. She just needs to fulfill her place in life…and *you* need to stay out of it!"

A vein stood out in anger in his already red forehead. Samantha was alarmed at what she saw, but continued.

"Plantation wives have no rights? No reason to be concerned when their husbands take their slave women and ignore their wives? Grady, you detest me!"

He glared at her.

"How dare you speak to me in that tone of voice! You're nothing but a spoiled Yankee! Ah truthfully don't know why ah married you!"

Without thinking, she slapped his arrogant face. In turn, he grabbed her arm and backhanded her as he shoved her. She flinched as her back hit the edge of the desk.

"Why don't you just go back up north? You certainly do not fit into my beloved south."

With that, Grady walked to the liquor cabinet and poured himself a drink.

Looking at him with disgust and painful emotion, she hurriedly left the room. Nothing would be the same ever again.

Samantha felt absolutely nothing as she watched Grady's big gray horse head down the lane from Hummingbird Hill to the battlefields.

7

The Battlefield 1863

Nathan

The smell of sulfur filled his nose until he couldn't breathe. Roar from cannons temporarily deafened him and the glare from cannonballs erupting nearby caused him to tightly close his eyes. He heard the call for retreat sounded and his mind told him to move but still he lay against the cold ground.

"Come on, Clevenger, let's get out of this mess," a seasoned soldier said, grabbing Nathan by the arm and dragging him to his feet.

They ran, hoping the enemy had exhausted their attack, hoping no stray bullet would find a mark on their backs as they ran. Having been on the front line, others joined them as they ran past the second line of defense and so forth until they were all safely behind the stone fence...that is, all except those who lay still and quiet on the battlefield. Men with smudges of gun powder and dirt on their faces and wild looks in their eyes were milling around, still feeling the adrenalin rush of the encounter with the enemy. Firearms were being routinely checked. That had to be the first concern...the firearms. Ever ready. Soldiers moved silently, trying desperately to believe they were the fortunate ones to have survived the latest barrage from the rebel forces. The bugler, riding back and forth through the lines on his horse, continued to sound retreat.

Little by little the word came down the line. The rebels had given up for now and had taken to the woods far beyond the line of battle. Things would settle down for the night and campfires on both sides would lend themselves to evening routines. But every man knew that would not be the end. The southern boys would regroup and attack again or the Yankees would pursue them, pushing them back, keeping them from advancing. Either way, it meant more fighting with even more gruesome results.

But before anyone satisfied the gnawing in their stomachs, roll would be taken and note would be made of those who did not return to the ranks of the survivors.

"You think there's anyone out there alive?" Nate whispered to the man next to him, gesturing towards the bodies that remained visible…those laying prone in the meadow that probably once had only felt the echo of gunshots from someone hunting for wild game.

"God, I sure hope not. Poor devils if they're still suffering."

At some point, a detail would be sent to gather the dead and give them as decent a burial as much as was possible under these conditions.

Nathan continued to clean his rifle. How in the world did he ever think he could make a difference? Just a year or two ago, he was in Washington plotting with Samantha and Chase to do some nonsensical thing. He didn't let his mind wander often to those days. It was too painful and emotional under the conditions of war. But tonight, the memories just kept gnawing at him.

"Let me try it."

"I would, Samantha; but if your father ever finds out, he would be furious. Girls just don't do those kinds of things," Nathan responded.

"I'll worry about my father. Just tell me what to do."

He resigned to her impetuousness.

"Okay, first you take a stance and then put the rifle to your shoulder, tight against your shoulder. Real tight. No, hold it straight. Sight down the barrel at the target."

"Alright, alright. Now can I shoot?" she was anxious.

"Just a minute," Nate said as he moved around her. "Let me check things out. Can you see the target?"

"Yes, now can I pull the trigger?"

She was filled with impatience.

Apparently satisfied she was doing what he'd asked, he continued.

"Just hang on a minute," he chided. "That's why girls don't handle guns. They shoot without thinking."

He was exhibiting a bit of impatience as well.

"Keep your eye on the target. Don't close your eyes."

"I'm ready."

"Now remember," he cautioned, "just squeeze the trigger. Anything else will move the gun and you'll shoot someone's leg off."

He smiled, but all the time thinking that was indeed a possibility.

But he hadn't time for more because, having waited long enough, she pulled the trigger. He jumped to the side as she lowered the rifle.

"I did it! I did it, Nate!" she squealed with delight. "I actually shot a gun!"

Without warning, she dropped the rifle to the ground as she threw her arms around him and kissed him.

That was Samantha...always full of life and enthusiasm.

Although he needed to chastise her for dropping the gun, instead his arms had automatically enfolded her and he wanted to continue to hold her. He decided against it.

"Yeah, you shot a rifle, but did you hit anything?" he laughed.

As they ran towards the target, he reached for her hand and she didn't object.

"See," she giggled. "Look, Nate, I did it."

"Well, I'll be darned," he said as he examined the bullet hole that had gone right through the middle of the target.

"Now, you'll never let me forget it, will you?" he joked, turning to look into her green eyes that danced with excitement.

"You got that right," she retorted, taking his arm as they made their way back across the field.

It was so comfortable to be with Nate and he was smart and good looking as well. She could picture herself with him and a house full of children and their families all coming to their house on the holidays. What a great life that would be!

She was comfortable to be with and her skin was like finest china. A beauty for sure. But not just on the outside. Samantha was a wonderful, caring, exciting girl and smart as a whip. Someday he'd ask her to marry him. His chest swelled at the thought.

"Thanks, Nate. You're the best!"

Nathan pushed the food around on the tin plate. Whatever this food was, it was neither good when it was hot or cold. But it kept them from starving. Supplies were in short demand and that in itself could win or lose the war. He wondered if Edward Stewart's business of supplying the troops was flourishing. No one thought this war would last this long. At first it had been full of expectation and enthusiasm. The union troops would march and push the southern troops back and a peace would be established and life would go on.

But then the cold of winter set in, the heat of summer, the lack of food, dysentery, blood, killing, dying, hunger, bodies that ached every morning from sleeping on the ground, fights breaking out within the campgrounds themselves. War was cruel and senseless and costly. But they were convinced just as much as the boys from the south that they were fighting for a cause. Did anyone even remember what the causes were anymore?

Nathan had seen his share of destruction and looting. Twice he had been shot and moved out of the front lines, but moved right back up as soon as he could move again. He had been a robust young man when he entered the war. Now his clothes hung on him and disappointment filled his eyes.

But tonight he was remembering Samantha...her gentleness and her creativeness. It was the only relief he knew to ease the reality of battle.

Teaching Samantha to shoot was only one of the many memories he had of her. When they were younger, she could outrun both Nate and Chase. As kids, they had built a fort and she had been involved in the building just as much as the boys. They played pranks on neighbors and enjoyed picnics and theater and carriage rides. They were good friends then, but they had grown up and their interests changed.

There was that winter she had asked him to take her to the cotillion. He had been reluctant.

"But you just have to take me," she coaxed. "You're the one who taught me how to dance and the only one I feel comfortable with."

It was true he had taught her to dance. His stressed patience proved that. She was not the most cooperative student, but the effort had been successful and he was delighted to spend any time with her.

She paused.

"Besides," she pouted, "father won't let Sinclair Samuels take me."

"Oh, I get it," he retaliated, "I'm a second choice, just someone to use so you can have your own way."

"Please don't look at it like that, Nathan," she begged, sensing he was beginning to weaken.

She walked away from him a bit.

"I suppose I could ask Chase to take me," she teased.

Whirling around, she attacked him again.

"But who wants to go to a fancy dance with their brother?"

Nathan wasn't finished. He was not willing to let it go.

"If I'm tied up with you, when do I have the chance to ask some sweet young girl to dance with me?"

She appeared puzzled by that remark, thinking carefully before she responded.

"Okay, I'll make you a deal" she decided. "You take me to the cotillion and dance with me...the first three dances; and if no one else asks me to dance, I'll just become a wallflower. Then you will be free to dance with whomever you please."

She put a little bit of tearful emotion in her voice for emphasis.

"Sounds reasonable," he teased, knowing she would rise to his challenge.

She put her hands on her hips as her green eyes flared at him.

"Just which girl are you talking about? Are you talking about Mary Louise Taylor?"

He threw his head back and laughed. She didn't pretend for long and joined him in the laughter.

"What put that smile on your face, Clevenger?" the soldier next to him asked.

Nathan smiled and shoveled another bit of food in his mouth.

"Thinking about home," he said wistfully.

"Aren't we all?" came the reply.

But Nathan Clevenger was lost the rest of the evening in his thoughts about Samantha Stewart. She had looked even more beautiful than ever at the cotillion. He remembered her gown as being green, the same color of green that matched the color of her eyes; and she certainly was the center of attention from the moment they entered the hall. They didn't even make it to dance number three before a line of young men was bidding to dance with her. Although he was not surprised, he reluctantly yielded and danced with several other young women; but his eyes were always on Samantha and he managed to cut in on several young men at various times.

It was the worst news of his entire life. Samantha...his Samantha...was being swept off her feet by some southerner. And now she had asked him to meet her down by the river. He paced back and forth in anticipation of her arrival.

"Nate," she yelled as she approached. "Nathan, over here!"

When she stepped from the carriage dressed in a pale blue summery gown with matching ribbons in her dark curls, he fought the mixture of feelings that threatened to overwhelm him.

As she hurried towards him, all he could think about was running to her and putting his arms around her and confessing what was in his heart. Reaching him, she embraced him and there were tears in her eyes when their eyes met.

"I wanted to be the first to tell you," she murmured.

"Tell me what?"

Perhaps if he avoided the rumors, they would not become reality.

"There's no easy way for me to say this."

"Then just come out with it," he encouraged. "We've never kept secrets from each other."

That was true. She had confided in him her deepest thoughts and he had always shared his feelings with her...well, all except this one he kept hidden.

Arm in arm, they turned and walked parallel to the Potomac. It was a lazy summer day and boats drifted on the water or chugged away carrying goods and passengers.

"I will miss this," she said wistfully.

"Then don't do it," he turned to her, almost begging.

She ignored his plea although she felt his arm tense under hers.

"The wedding is set for the first day of July," she continued. "Grady needs to get back to the plantation. It seems the most convenient way to go about things."

They walked in silence.

"I want you to be happy," he finally said.

"You will come see me, won't you?" she pleaded, choking back the emotion she felt.

"Oh, I don't know, Samantha," he replied. "I would have to consider the wisdom of that."

He saw the disappointment in her face. How could he deny her anything?

"We'll see. Maybe," he added.

Once again her face was alive.

"Come when the magnolias are in bloom. I hear it's beautiful at that time of year."

They continued their walk, neither one of them willing to leave the other.

For a brief instant in the silence of the battlefield before he fell asleep, he was holding her once again as they glided across the floor at the cotillion. She was looking into his eyes and smiling and she felt so good in his arms.

Tired as he was, Nathan had a rather fitful night, dreaming of Samantha, wondering if she indeed was happy being the wife of a rich plantation owner.

8

Somewhere Near the North Carolina Border
1864

Chase

If he had his bearings correct and from what he could tell, Chase had made it safely through Virginia and its many battlefields. Crossing over into North Carolina did not make his journey any safer, but it brought him that much closer to Samantha. But the journey thus far had taken its toll. He had lost a considerable amount of weight and the wounded shoulder caused him pain every day. He was hungry most of the time and wild game seemed to be in demand these days. But there were many men who needed food in order to survive these times of struggle. He found himself frequently thinking of his mother's bountiful table and the comfort of their home in Washington.

But thoughts of home and mother who lay on her sick bed were not comforting and prodded him to focus on his reason for this journey…to bring Samantha home safely to their mother who lay ill in Washington, D. C. He momentarily stopped to pray for his mother's wellbeing. Once again, urgency overtook him.

Mountainous areas made for slow going. But he pushed forward, carefully skirting battles, sometimes laying low for several days at a time until he was sure either union or confederate forces were moving on.

He was pretty sure he had remained vigilant, necessity being the major factor. But on this particular day, he had misread the signs, somehow disregarded what he knew to be true. One moment he was winding his way through heavy brush and the next he was surrounded by four men on horseback.

"State yore business!" the man who seemed to have seniority demanded.

Chase immediately put his hands where they could be seen.

"I am a single man traveling to see my sister in South Carolina."

By the look on the men's faces, he was pretty sure they doubted that statement.

"Sir, are you a spy for the union military?"

"No, sir, I have told you the truth."

"Please dismount," the soldier demanded.

Chase was very uncomfortable, wondering the wisdom of following orders; but since there were four of them and one of him, he did what was asked. One of the men also dismounted; and pulling Chase's arms around to his back, causing the injured shoulder to wrench with pain which shot down his arm, proceeded to tie his wrists. He felt the security of his gun being removed from his belt and the cold steel blade of his knife leaving its place next to his leg. A sharp jab in the middle of Chase's back signaled he should start walking. If he slowed, he was prodded to keep up. By the time the sun was directly overhead and beating down unmercifully, they were still walking.

"Water," Chase whispered as he trudged along.

He was ignored.

By the time they arrived at the encampment, he estimated it must have been partly through the afternoon. Disgruntled men gaped at him on either side and threw insults at him as he was paraded towards a tent he assumed was that of the commander. The soldier who had first talked to him, muttered something at the flap of the tent and a lieutenant emerged.

A flurry of conversation between the lieutenant and the soldier who had brought Chase in only resulted in the lieutenant retreating back into the tent while sweat poured down Chase's face as he stood in the blazing heat. While the remaining three soldiers left to return to their normal routines, Chase looked around him at the camp which appeared to be a camp just like others he'd observed. A few men were in uniform, but mostly the soldiers were in tattered regular clothing. Southern accents pierced the air. Clearly this was a confederate camp. Small camp fires for cooking were located in several places, some men were sleeping, some playing cards, others talking. All looked at him suspiciously. The smell of food cooking caused his stomach to lurch and he wondered how long it had been since he had eaten.

"Commander's busy right now," the lieutenant reported. "Just leave him tied and put him over there near that tree."

Mulling over the possibilities of the delay being either in his favor or a bad omen, Chase staggered as the soldier grunted and nudged Chase in the direction of a nearby tree where he collapsed on the ground, finally wiggling around to a sitting position still with his hands tied behind his back.

"Could I please have a drink of water?" he asked.

At first he thought he might be refused again, but then the soldier grabbed a tin cup from a pile of them lying on the ground and scooped some water from an open bucket and handed him a drink.

"Thank you," Chase said humbly and gratefully.

It would be the last gesture of kindness he would encounter for some time.

Chase dozed in the heat of the afternoon, being tired from the march he was forced to make and from the long days of travel since he'd left Washington and too little food.

He slept fitfully, frequently dreaming of his father standing in front of him telling him this journey would not be an easy one. For a few moments he resented Clinton and Edward back home with the comfort of family. Visions of his mother lamenting over Samantha's absence and fearing for Samantha's wellbeing danced before his eyes. He *had* to bring Samantha back to their ailing mother.

"Stand up, soldier!"

He heard the command but could not respond out of his lethargic state.

"Ah said stand up, soldier!"

The voice was louder this time.

He felt someone take him by the shoulder and haul him to his feet. He staggered a bit, still foggy from interrupted sleep. A ruddy faced man with large hands steadied him.

"State yore name, soldier."

This from the tall slender man in uniform with piercing eyes and graying beard who stood directly before him. He saw by the decorations on his shoulder that this was probably the senior officer in the camp.

Chase mustered all the courage he could find as the world once again seemed to come into focus.

"Sir, I am not a soldier," he said.

He said it with all meekness and respect, but fire flew in the commander's eyes as if he had indeed been challenged. A pair of leather gloves the commander had previously held in his hands flew across Chase's face.

"Do not disrespect me, son," he yelled.

"State yore name and yore business."

"I am Chase Stewart from Washington, D. C. I am on my way to see my sister in South Carolina."

"A likely story, suh," the lieutenant spoke. "Do not disrespect Commander Clyde."

Chase moved his head slightly to see the young lieutenant standing at the side of the commander.

"Not a story," Chase defended. "I'm telling you the truth."

The commander once again engaged him in conversation.

"I pray you are telling the truth. At any rate, we will find out if you are a union spy. We have our ways. And if you are," his voice deepened, "it will not go well with you."

Apparently the commander had donated enough time to this issue and needed to focus on more important ones. Turning, he spoke to the ruddy faced man.

"Keep him tied up, Barnes. To a tree. No food or water. We'll find out what he knows. He'll be glad to talk. He's weak. It shouldn't take long."

With that, the commander strode back to his tent, the ever-present lieutenant by his side. Barnes moved Chase to a more permanent place against a tree. Here Chase would not be able to sit down. Barnes went about his task silently, refusing to look Chase in the eyes. Finally, feeling as if the prisoner was secure, he spoke.

"The commander don't take kin'ly ta spies," he said and then walked away, not waiting for or interested in a response.

Not only were Chase's hands bound tightly now but he also had a rope around his shoulders which extended around the tree and kept him immobile. Rough bark from the tree dug into his back. He tried to concentrate on the parts of his body that he could move...consciously taking periods of time to exercise his feet, shuffling them back and forth in place, flexing his leg muscles. But his neck and shoulders began to ache. Pain went right to the injured shoulder. Moving his head from side to side in an effort to ease the pain did not work. He tried hard to concentrate on the layout of the camp and keep his mind active, but his thoughts continued to return to the commander's words *It shouldn't take too long.* If there was a weakness anywhere, Chase needed to find it.

To his right was the commander's tent, headquarters for this unit. To his left some distance away was a stream of water...not a large one, perhaps adequate for the needs of a few, not likely adequate for a group this large. From what he could tell, his back was to the edge of the camp. He didn't think he sensed any activity behind him. Straight in front of him were a few small tents and the remains of campfires. Farther beyond the commander's tent was a small herd of horses including the one Chase had been riding. He surmised most of the men here were foot soldiers. Southern accents drifted across the late afternoon as men conversed although Chase was too far away to make out more than a word or two here and there.

He pulled against his restraints, but there was no give in them. Barnes had been thorough, but then why wouldn't he be? If a prisoner escaped due to his inefficiency, he surely would be the one to be punished.

Night fell and Chase could no longer see movement in the camp. A harmonica wailed a mournful tune and then all was silent. Chase fought with himself to keep his mind active and on positive things, but his thoughts always came back to how he could possibly convince Commander Clyde that he was not a spy, just a brother in search of his sister.

When he dozed, his body weight pulled against the restraints and woke him. By morning, he was exhausted...exactly what the commander had hoped for. Chase figured it must be half past the morning by the time Barnes came for him. This time, Chase was released from the tree and his hands were untied. He enjoyed the freedom and began to move and rub his hands and arms and shoulder as he was escorted once again before the commander.

"Mr. Stewart, I trust that you might be ready to tell us the truth."

Chase considered lying, but did not think that would further his cause any more than telling the truth.

"My name is Chase Stewart. I am from Washington, D. C. I am on my way to South Carolina to visit my sister."

Commander Clyde paced in front of him. Then he turned with fury.

"You are a spy for the union forces and you have penetrated our lines to obtain information which you'all intend to take back to the union commands."

"No, I am not!" Chase objected. Then quickly added, "Sir."

The commander nodded at the lieutenant.

Stepping forward, the lieutenant struck Chase in the stomach with his left fist. As Chase doubled with the pain, the lieutenant's right hand came up under Chase's chin and Chase felt his head snap. His first inclination was to retaliate when Barnes grabbed him from behind while the lieutenant landed several well placed jabs to Chase's face, bringing new blood to fresh cuts.

With a wave of his hand, the commander indicated that was enough for now.

Chase groaned as Barnes led him away to the same tree, bending over periodically to spit blood on the ground from his split lip. This time, Chase was tied with his face towards the tree and his arms tied around the tree. He could see nothing; and with his face against the rough bark of the tree, any movement of his head permitted renewed fresh pain to return to the raw cuts. He tasted blood from the wounds as it oozed into his mouth. His right eye stung and throbbed. All through the day he passed in and out of consciousness.

The sun was just going down over the mountain when Barnes appeared and untied him so he could relieve himself; and he was offered a cup of water and a biscuit that was hard enough to be labeled as ammunition. But it was food and he relished in it, savoring each bite.

"You got family?" Chase slurred through his bleeding lip.

At first, Chase thought Barnes was going to deny conversation.

"Yeah," he said in low tones. "A wife and two kids."

"Bet you miss them," Chase pursued, squinting at him through the swollen eye.

Barnes was quiet for a long time.

"Yep," he finally said and then turned and walked away.

The second day was worse than the first. Chaos descended on the camp as something had set off one of the soldiers and he went berserk and had to be restrained. Apparently new orders had come through because the camp seemed to be in a state of agitation preparing to move. And with all the confusion, perhaps Commander Clyde had forgotten the prisoner in camp. If these were confederate troops, they would probably be moving north...the opposite direction from where Chase needed to be.

At that point, Chase considered the possibility of being shot. After all, now he was extra baggage to Commander Clyde and the troops. A bargaining chip perhaps. He considered the possibilities of using that bit of information to his advantage. One way or another, a man suspected of spying would not be kept around long. All of his thoughts focused on his escape.

Barnes evidently was the one who was going to be saddled with Chase's care. He released Chase from the tree, tying one end of the rope around Chase's waist and the other end of the rope around his own waist. Evidently they were to be best buddies on this trip. A grateful Chase accepted his good fortune. As they walked, Chase listened carefully to everything he heard, especially if the words came from either the lieutenant or Commander Clyde. He needed to know what the orders were and if there was anything in those plans he could use as a means of escape.

"Two kids, eh?" Chase ventured. "Boys or girls?"

Barnes was not supposed to talk to the prisoner. He could be reprimanded for such an infraction of the rules. And Chase understood that so he remained quiet and waited.

"One of each," came the answer some minutes later.

Chase looked at Barnes out of the corner of his swollen eye. There was emotion in the soldier's face.

"How old?"

Barnes struggled with the thought of his children somewhere miles away from him.

"Boy's ten. Girl's eight."

Chase let that settle in for a while. When he thought it safe, he ventured more conversation.

"Sounds about right for me and my sister. Our mother is very ill and I've been sent to fetch my sister home before anything happens to our mother."

There was no further comment from Barnes. As Chase studied Barnes' face, he thought perhaps Barnes was considering everything Chase had said.

After a reasonable amount of time, Chase picked up the subject again.

"Imagine your boy has become the man of the house."

"Yup."

"The protector of the family. You worry about them much? Well, of course you do. You out here in the middle of nowhere and them back home. Where's home?"

"Mississippi."

"That's a far piece."

"Yup."

Chase let it rest and trudged on with the rest of the weary men. They had covered more miles than he cared to think about and his feet hurt; but in his mind, it was one step better than being tied to a tree. Or worse yet, dead. However, when camp was made for the evening, he was once again tied to a tree. He almost hoped that with the orders Commander Clyde had received, he would forget about the prisoner; but that was not the case. The lieutenant seemed to enjoy his job of doling out punishment and Chase received new bruises and cuts and older ones were reopened. With visions of infection and Mac still prominent in his head, his story remained the same. His name was Chase Stewart and he was from Washington, D. C. and was going south to visit his sister.

He saw the surprise in Barnes' face the next morning when he came to secure him once again to his waist. Chase could hardly see out of his right eye. He felt every ache as Barnes pulled him to his feet.

"The lieutenant again?" Barnes whispered.

Chase nodded his head.

Looking around to see that they were not being watched, Barnes slipped a piece of fat back and a Johnnie cake into Chase's hands. Not willing that Barnes get should into trouble for his action, Chase fought back his desire to gobble the food, but took his time, chewing discreetly when no one was looking.

Chase thought perhaps he had all but been forgotten on day two of the march. He found time for more conversation with Barnes, finding out that Barnes was indeed a good and compassionate man. Talk of his family seem to be the chink in Barnes' armor, perhaps Chase's one chance of using that in an effort to get out of his imprisonment.

That evening, after Chase had been secured to yet another tree, he was surprised to find there was some give in the ropes that confined him. A mistake? An error? Intentional? He was at the edge of the encampment, quite a few yards away from the troops. Working carefully at the rope, he managed to get one hand free. It was an exhilarating feeling...realizing the chance that lay before him. But what if he were caught? Perhaps it would be better to play along for a time. No, the chance might never come again. As long as Commander Clyde thought he was spying for the union, he would be in danger of being shot or hung. Indeed, he was extremely fortunate that hadn't happened already. He guessed it would be better if he was shot making a dash for freedom rather than waiting for a formal execution.

Pretending to be sleeping, he watched the night patrol walk past. The soldier on guard duty kicked Chase in the leg as he passed and Chase stirred as if he were still asleep. He breathlessly counted the minutes in between their visits and allowed there would be at least fifteen minutes for him to get as far as he could before the next watch came by and his escape would be found out. Then his absence would be discovered and the chase would be on. How far could he get in fifteen minutes? Hopefully it would be far enough. But what of Barnes? He most assuredly would be in big trouble for letting a prisoner escape. But after all, he had intentionally left the bonds loosen, hadn't he? Even if he hadn't, could Chase afford not to take advantage of the opportunity? It even occurred to him that he may have been set up. Shooting a fleeing prisoner would be a valid excuse. The answer always came back as a *no.* He would take the chance. Still positioned as if he were tied, he waited breathlessly for the next watch to pass by. His anticipation was at an all-time high as he heard the night guard approach. Waiting until he heard the footsteps grow fainter, he then took the opportunity to scramble to his feet, taking the rope with him.

Desperately trying to make as little noise as possible, he disappeared into the night, away from the dim campfire light, running as fast as his body would tolerate. His breath came in short gasps because of his weakened condition. It didn't take him long to tire and then he heard the commotion in the camp behind him. He tensed even more and a crawling sensation moved up his back. His absence had been discovered. And they were coming faster than he had anticipated. Men on horseback would cover distance more quickly than a man on foot.

Panic set in as an overwhelming feeling that he would not be able to outrun them enveloped him.

"Hey, Chase, come on, we can outrun them," Nathan said as the two teenage boys raced through an orchard at the edge of Washington, D. C.

"You're insane," Chase answered. *"If you hadn't provoked them, we wouldn't be running for our lives."*

"The tree," Nathan panted. *"We can get above them and let them pass right on by."*

"I can't do that," Chase panted. *"I can't climb that high."*

"Yes, you can," Nathan encouraged. *"I know you can. Give it a try!"*

That was it! *Thank you, Nathan.* Chase looked around in a panic. It was difficult to see in the dark, but he could barely make out the outline of a tree. He grabbed for the lowest limb and missed. Backing away from the tree, he ran and with all the strength he could summon, finally feeling the coarseness of the limb in his hands. Swinging his weight for momentum, he clawed and felt the weight of his body straining against his hands and arms. At one point, he thought he did not have enough strength left to follow through. But slowly his muscles began to function to pull him up to the safety of the first limb. Fresh scrapes opened up on his hands and legs. Reaching for the next limb, he found it closer than he had anticipated. Was it far enough to not be seen? Too late to move any further? He heard the sounds of the horses pounding the earth. He sat crouched, hugging the trunk of the tree and fearing that even the noise of his breathing would give him away.

They stopped right below him at the base of the tree; and he heard a lot of shouting, heard the snort of the horses as they pranced, eager to get on with the hunt. They seemed to mill around beneath the tree, deep in conversation which was indistinguishable to him. Then came the overwhelming sensation that they were giving up the search. He waited. He waited a long time after the sound of the soldiers on horseback were no longer detected. Silence descended once again in the night air. Only then did he feel comfortable enough to move to the bottom limb and then jump to the ground.

He nearly lost his balance as he hit the ground. Turning around and starting to run, he was stopped short when he felt the cold steel against the back of his head.

"Stay right where you are," came the voice from behind him.

Chase's hands automatically reached upward.

9

Hummingbird Hill, December 1861

Samantha

Cooler December weather brought thoughts of Christmas to Hummingbird Hill. Samantha placed homemade candles on the fireplace mantles and surrounded them with green boughs and looped them with red and gold ribbon she had purchased on their trip to Charleston that first year they were married. She sat down in a rocking chair to observe her handiwork; and in a moment of peacefulness, she fell asleep.

"Hurry, Samantha," mother called from the foot of the stairs. "Grandmother and Grandfather Chase will be here soon and you aren't even out of bed."

Samantha woke to the most delicious of smells emanating from the kitchen. And then the realization...this was Christmas Day. That meant lots of food to eat, lots of company and presents. Such an exciting day!

"Coming, mother," she called down as she struggled into her best gown for the day's festivities.

Samantha had spent the last few weeks making gifts and surprises for this day and she was eager to see them opened and enjoyed. Guests and relatives would be coming and going throughout the day to bring good wishes and to give and receive gifts, each one enjoying a glass of mother's famous hot punch and tea cakes.

Christmas was a splendid day.

Samantha awoke from her reverie of Christmas past. Well, this Christmas would be fine here at Hummingbird Hill with or without Grady Reynolds. She was healthy and had plenty to eat so she was more fortunate than those who were spending Christmas on the battlefields.

But the dream of home and Christmas and family had sparked thoughts that weren't easily put aside and surfaced again in her dreams that evening.

"I am so excited, mother!" Samantha said as she approved of the dining room table laden with food.

"Well, you should be," Claudia Stewart was very proud of her gorgeous and only daughter. "It isn't every day a young lady turns sixteen years old."

"And I love my new dress," Samantha gushed as she smoothed the folds of the green silk gown trimmed with cream colored lace.

She made a couple of turns in the hallway to demonstrate its qualities.

"I am so glad Father has consented to permitting the dance and allowed me to invite my friends."

"Well, you are your father's pride and joy," Claudia Stewart shared. "But remember your manners. After all, you are a young woman now. You need to be a gracious hostess."

Strains of music floated over the hall in the Stewart home as eight young people enjoyed refreshments and dancing. Laughter penetrated every corner of the room. Samantha looked around the room for Nathan. Other young men had asked her to dance, but where was Nathan? She spied him in the corner talking with Chase. She made her way towards the two young men.

"Dance with me, Nathan," she begged.

"Is that a requirement for all who attend your parties?" he teased.

"Oh, just come on," she said as she led him by the arm to the dance floor.

"Might as well," Chase teased as he placed his hand on Nathan's shoulder. "There'll be no peace around here if she doesn't get her way. But I guess it is her birthday after all."

Samantha screwed up her face at her brother's comments, but readily accepted Nathan's extended hand.

Being in Nathan's arms was about as natural a feeling as she had ever known. He held her lightly, but was masterful in his leading. But, he had been the one who had spent many laborious hours teaching her the art.

"It's quite warm in here, don't you think?" she said as she looked up into his eyes.

"Would you like to go outside on the balcony?" he asked.

"Yes," she smiled. "Yes, let's."

Nathan followed her to the balcony into the coolness of the night air.

"Isn't this just the most wonderful night, Nathan?" she glowed.

"Yes," he answered, admiring her exuberance. "It's a wonderful party, Samantha."

They looked out over the gardens that glistened in the moonlight.

"Thank you for coming," she said as she turned towards him.

"I wouldn't have missed it for anything," he said sincerely. "Well, unless there was a really good reason like another invitation or the guys wanted me to go hunting or…"

"Stop teasing me, Nathan," she pouted. "You know you want to be here."

Nathan stepped closer to her.

"Yes, Samantha," he said softly. "I want to be here with you. I want to celebrate all the memorable moments of your life."

She stared into his eyes as he reached into his pocket and produced a small package.

"Ooh, for me?"

Samantha was always eager to receive gifts and Nathan had been giving her birthday presents since she was ten years old. She readily opened the box to reveal a small silver ring.

"Oh, Nathan," she gasped.

He saw the incredible look in her eyes and she was standing so close to him and the dress revealed her shoulders and she was so wonderful. So he did the only thing he could do. He put his arms around her and found the softness of her lips.

She was shocked to find herself kissing him as well.

He continued to hold her.

"Happy sixteenth birthday, Samantha," he whispered.

Samantha woke with a start and her hand went immediately to her lips. It had been so real that she could actually smell the cologne he wore, feel the tingle from his kiss. She looked around the room and settled back against her pillow as she pulled the sheets up around her and tried to catch her breath.

She woke early the next morning looking for the box, positive she had brought it with her from Washington. Yes, she was sure of it. But where? She sorted through drawers and then raced to find the travel trunk. Yes, that's where it would be. And sure enough, there was the treasured wooden box which held all of Nathan's gifts.

Upon opening it, a wave of nostalgia passed through her. Treasures from Nathan. There was the note from him, the one he'd given her on her 10th birthday written in his own hand. *Happy Birthday to my best friend, Samantha Stewart from Nathan Clevinger.* It was accompanied by his best rendition of a red rose.

She smiled. She knew every gift from memory. Her eleventh birthday gift was the collection of small sea shells he had brought her after his family had gone to the seashore. Number twelve was the gold coin; thirteen, the lace handkerchief; fourteen, the china cup and saucer; fifteenth, the small journal to write her innermost thoughts and in which he had written that she needed to show him its contents when she turned twenty five. And then the sixteenth birthday was the silver ring…and her first kiss.

Frantically pushing past the other treasures, she searched until she found the silver ring on the silver chain. Carefully removing it from its place in the corner of the box, she took a deep breath, remembering the night of her sixteenth birthday party when he had given it to her. Slipping it over her neck, it fell next to her grandmother's locket. Touching it gently, tears formed in her eyes.

How she missed Nathan and the feeling of security she experienced when she was with him.

A few days after Grady rode off with Jed and Luke Prescott to join other southerners in the war, Samantha made her way to his room and found the box which contained the keys she had seen him place there. On this December day, she concealed them in the pocket of her dress as she crept down the stairway to the library and unlocked the drawer to the huge oak desk…the drawer where plantation records were kept. She studied the books with great interest, noting the quantity of cotton the plantation had sold at market and the amount of profit, how much seed had cost and when it was planted and harvested.

But of the most interest was the record book on the slaves. Each slave was listed individually and a monetary value was entered on the same line, male slaves being much more valuable than female slaves.

But there was one section in the book that dealt entirely with female slaves. Each name was entered, followed by an age, a date, a child's name and a birth date for that child. Scanning the pages, she found names of slaves she recognized and names of some slaves that had been sold off. Two names stood out in Samantha's mind. One was that of Clover. She traced her finger across the page. Son, Samuel, born April, 1853. Son, Isaiah, born May, 1855. Son, Esau, born June 1857. Son, Adam, born July 1859, shortly after Samantha's arrival at Hummingbird Hill. The last birth had been a girl, Aseneth, born in September this year 1861. It was clear the second date was the birth of the child. There were many other dates under Clover's name but no other children listed. What of those dates?

She continued down the page until she came to Izzy's name followed by a date of March, 1861.

Callie bursting through the library doors caused her to leave the books laying open on the desk.

"Come quick, Ms. Samantha," she called, being out of breath from her haste.

"What is it, Callie?"

"It's Izzy! She be askin' fer you."

Samantha needed no further information. It was time for Izzy's baby to be born. Grabbing her shawl, she followed Callie's well rounded body through the kitchen and across the yard to the slave cabins. Slave women had been having babies for centuries without the help of anyone else, but Izzy was special.

In the two years she had been at Hummingbird Hill, Samantha had never once been inside the slave quarters. The first things she became aware of was a distinct odor and the soft glow from wood burning in the fireplace although it hadn't made much progress against the cold of December. She felt the softness of the dirt floor under her feet. A small amount of light from a lone window on one side of the cabin permeated the darkness. When her eyes became adjusted, she focused on the crude bed where Izzy lay.

"It will be alright, Izzy," she murmured as she picked up the girl's frail hand in hers. "This will be alright."

Callie and Miriam worked quietly, encouraging Izzy's frail body through the entire process.

Izzy's moans increased as the labor pains increased, making it easy for Callie and Miriam to monitor the progress of the birth.

When they became intense, Izzy strained and her tiny arms pulled against the branches of wood that formed the head of the bed.

"Ah don't want this baby," Izzy screamed.

"Of course you do," Samantha attempted to comfort. "This will be over soon and you will have a beautiful baby."

Callie and Miriam exchanged glances and kept right on with their work.

It was several hours later when Izzy's baby finally arrived, a tiny baby girl, a beautiful little girl.

Izzy cried when they told her and refused to look at the child.

Callie held the bundle close to her motherly body and crooned a soft tune. Miriam sat on the side of the bed.

"Ah knows how you feel, Izzy," she soothed. "Ah won't promise you thet it'll get easier; but this baby, well, she be a child of God and His creation. In this ole world, she gonna need her mama."

Samantha took the wrinkled bundle from Callie and placed the little girl next to Izzy in the bed. Izzy turned her face away.

"What shall we name her?" Samantha asked, trying to understand Izzy's rejection of the baby.

"Ya'all gives her a name," Izzy sobbed.

Samantha was quiet as she stroked Izzy's forehead in a calming manner.

"Let's call her Hope," she finally said. "Hope for the future."

Izzy shook her head in agreement and turned away and sobbed again.

Samantha stood and made her way to the cabin door, opening it to the light of the cold December day. Izzy's husband, John, stood near the door.

"You have a baby girl," Samantha said.

She had always known Izzy's John to be a peaceable man, but the anger she saw in his eyes was bewildering to her.

"Congratulations."

Almost as if he hadn't heard the words, he asked, "Izzy be alright?"

"She's fine," Samantha replied. "A little emotional right now, but fine."

John opened the door and entered the slave cabin.

Pulling her shawl tighter around her shoulders, Samantha made her way back into the house. Once again she poured over the record books in the library. She entered today's date on the line next to Izzy's name and wrote *Female, Hope* next to it. Glancing backwards, she looked again at the first date on the line…March, 1861. Samantha's stomach became nauseous with the realization as she recalled the events of last March and fully comprehended what had taken place. In her mind, she could still see Grady striding across the yard to the slave quarters. Anger rose within her.

It was time for the mistress of Hummingbird Hill to carve out her own path.

10

Northern North Carolina,
1864

Chase

Change. Change beyond imagination. When Chase left the security of his home in Washington, D. C., he viewed himself as a healthy young man with a relatively positive outlook on life. Now he was tired and hungry most of the time and his injured shoulder was in constant pain. His beard was scraggly and his hair was greasy. Scars from his recent beatings were not yet healed. His horse was now a permanent part of some confederate regiment. Things he once had taken so much patience in packing into his saddlebags including his gun and knife had all been confiscated as well as most of the money he had. Only a small amount, well-hidden in the heel of his boot, had eluded his captures. Perhaps the soldier who searched him had been less thorough in his haste to attend to other matters.

And now he had escaped the clutches of the confederate army by taking refuge in a tree. But just as he thought he'd made good on his escape, he found himself confronted once more.

"Don't move," the voice came from behind him.

Chase had no intention of moving.

Once again, Chase felt the hair on the back of his neck raise. He slowly lifted his hands, the rope from his escape still secure in the right one. As he did, he whirled around, lashing out with the rope and catching the man by surprise. The most he could tell in the darkness was that the man was of stocky build and reeked of tobacco and liquor. Soldier? Chase didn't know. He just knew that he put the piece of rope around the man's neck and held it tight until he felt the body slump. Not knowing if the man was alive or not, he slipped the rope from around his neck and started at a dead run to put more space between him and the scene.

He hoped the skirmish had not piqued the interest of the Johnny Rebs into coming back to once again search the area. Whether they would take the time the following morning or not he did not know. Hopefully they had more important things on their minds than to pursue a suspected spy. He would continue to wonder, but he would wonder from a place as far away from here as he could find.

It didn't take long for his run to slow to a walk. He was weakened from lack of food and his feet were sore from being forced to keep up the pace with the troops the past few days. Still he knew he needed to keep moving and he hoped he was moving in a southerly direction. When the first rays of sun came up over the mountains, he was convinced he was once again headed south. A crevice carved out from part of the mountainside looked like a good place to rest; and breaking some branches from a nearby pine tree to cover himself, he curled up and slept until he was awakened by the sound of horses' hooves. An army was once again on the move. He watched from his vantage point and drew in a deep breath, convinced they were far enough away to overlook his hiding place.

He walked slowly throughout the day, keeping an eye out for anything he might find to eat. No food. No weapons other than the rope he still carried. No means to build a fire. Indeed, life for Chase Stewart seemed bleak at best. He grazed on nuts and berries when he could find them and tried to stay near creeks and rivers when he could. But he also knew that both sides in the war would do the same.

Was this to be the end for him? Starving to death, alone and away from home?

Coming upon a clearing, he spotted a small cabin nestled among a grove of trees. He watched for hours for any sign of activity. Seeing none, he proceeded cautiously until he was within a few yards of the door. He noted a lean to of sorts had been built on the side of the cabin where obviously some kind of animal was stabled. Once again scanning the clearing and feeling confident no one was there, he made his way to the door and opened it. One room. A table. And food! Fresh biscuits were on the table and he picked several up at one time and began to cram them into his empty stomach.

He heard the sound of the gun being readied before he heard the words.

"Need sum milk with them biscuits?"

Chase turned to look into the eyes of a young woman dressed in britches and flannel shirt, wearing a wide brimmed hat pulled down tight on her head.

He stopped part way through a mouthful of biscuit and stared right into the barrel of the gun she held.

"You cain't talk?" she asked.

"Sorry," he answered. "It's been a long time since I've had anything to eat."

It was a simple clarification but one he felt needed to be said to explain his actions.

She temporarily lowered the gun, careful not to turn her back on him. Reaching for the pail of milk she had set down at the door with one hand, she kept the gun at the ready with the other.

"I wasn't joshin' 'bout the milk," she said, heaving the bucket to the table and reaching to remove a tin cup from the shelf behind her with her free hand.

He stood immobile as if he had just seen an angel of mercy.

"You got a name?" she asked, shoving the cup of milk towards him with one hand, keeping the weapon ready with the other.

"Chase," he murmured in between gulps of milk. "Thank you."

She seemed to ignore his gratitude. But she hadn't overlooked his gaunt appearance and the hunger in his eyes.

"Better take it easy on the food if'n ya haven't eaten much. Belly takes some gettin' used to after bein' starved."

She gestured towards a straight chair for him and pulled up a small crude bench across from him. He sat down as well. She laid the gun across the small table within easy reach.

"So, Chase, whut brings you by here? You union or rebel?"

"Neither," he explained. "I am on my way to South Carolina. My sister is there and I aim to take her back to Washington, D. C."

"Thet seems a might foolish," her eyes squinted showing her disbelief. " 'Specially with the war an' all."

She paused.

"Ya did know a war wuz goin' on, didn't ya?"

Chase was too tired to do much more than nod.

"My sister...Samantha's her name...she married a man from South Carolina, but our mother has taken gravely ill and I have been sent to bring Samantha back to her."

They sat in silence.

"Samantha's a purty name. I'm Oma. Jest plain Oma. You look like you could use some rest."

Chase nodded his head again.

"We can talk tomorrow," Oma said. "There's the loft and here's a blanket."

She nodded towards the ladder that went up to the loft and Chase was grateful. Exhaustion overtook him and he was fast asleep before Oma had fed the livestock.

He woke with a start, temporarily forgetting where he was. The aroma of food cooking was a pleasant surprise to his stomach. Throwing aside the blanket, he climbed down the ladder. Oma was at the cook stove stirring eggs in a black iron skillet. Remembering her feistiness at the time of his arrival, he was quite sure she could use the frying pan as a weapon if necessary.

" 'Mornin'," he said.

Obviously Oma had been up long before he heard her stirring.

She looked up from her task and grunted a reply. Nothing else was said until she scooped half of the contents of the skillet onto a tin plate and shoved it in front of him. Eggs and fresh biscuits. Certainly a feast for hungry bodies.

"What's yer story?" she proposed, having felt he had temporarily satisfied his stomach.

"My name is Chase Stewart. I'm on my way to South Carolina to take my sister back to Washington, D. C."

"Yeah," her blue eyes sparkled. "Thet's whut ya said last night."

"Well, since I left home, I've lost practically everything I started out with and have encountered danger from both sides of this war."

She shook her head.

"Ah ain't got much, but you kin stay here fer a bit if you like an' rest up sum. Ah watch the movement of the soldiers and ah think it's safe here fer a while. They don't cum 'round here much."

"Surely there is something I can do for you to repay your kindness," he offered.

"I al'ays got chores. Finish up yer breakfast and we'll see what we can find to do."

He scooped up the last bite of eggs and crammed yet another biscuit into his mouth, washed it down with a full cup of milk and followed her out the door. Yes, there would be plenty to do here. And besides, a few days rest would be a welcome benefit.

Two days turned into three and then four and more. Under Oma's careful guidance, they were able to catch some wild game.

"I know whur they hide," she explained. "They don't like all the commotion of the soldiers passin' through and certainly don't like no gunfire."

Chase split wood and gained some strength in his shoulder. He was able to take a bath and Oma washed his clothes and gave him a spare shirt that had belonged to her father. She was a fair cook and had a little vegetable garden growing out back which added to her meager diet.

She heard it before he was even aware anyone was around.

"Shh," she cautioned. "Someone's a comin'."

Chase listened to hear what Oma was hearing. Sure enough, before long Chase saw a blue uniform out the tiny window. Union soldiers!

"Ya'all git up in the loft," she said as she grabbed her shotgun and opened the front door.

Chase listened from his hiding place. No, no there hadn't been anybody around the place for days. Oma was convincing and the small detail of union soldiers were on their way.

"Thanks," Chase said as he made his way down the ladder.

"Ah spect ya ain't no threat to no one," she replied as she once again placed the shotgun in its spot near the door. " 'Sides, ya'all bin good ter me."

"How is it you live here all alone, Oma?" he asked as he sat across the table from her.

She finished the mouthful of food and took time to lay down her spoon as if she were trying to remember the circumstances.

"Mah Paw and Maw built this place. Ah was born right hehr. Ain't never been no further then over ta town twenty miles away...and thet only to git supplies. Indians used to be in this part of the country. They wuz friendly and let us live hehr in peace. Maw took sick and died when ah was ten. Paw and me kept workin' the place. He talked 'bout movin' on, but he ne'er wanted ta leave Maw buried here all alone. So we stayed. Ah hain't ne'er knowed anythin' else. Then Paw up and died 'bout two year ago so ah jest stay hehr now, too."

There may have been a slight wistfulness in her voice.

"Don't you ever get lonely?" Chase sympathized.

"Oh, sure, sometimes," she answered, "but ah guess ya git used ter bein' alone and hit's okay."

She gazed absently out the window.

"It's a purty place...the mountains and the crick. Yep, purty place...jest like Paw said."

"But how do you make a living?"

"Don't need much," her answer was sure. "Ah got the cow and ah raise a hog or two fer food. Sell the rest of the litter off to a feller who cums by onct a year. Thet gives me money to get supplies. Ever'thin' else iz off the land."

"You seem happy, Oma," Chase said, suddenly feeling the absence of his own family.

They were quiet.

"You leavin', ain't ya?"

"I have to," Chase admitted. "It's time to move on. Remember…my sister…"

"I 'member."

She was quiet again.

"Ya needs ta find yer sister. Ah hope ya do. Samantha's a real purty name."

By the time Chase awoke the following morning, Oma had a knapsack full of food for his journey.

"Don't have much, but this'll get you by," she said shyly.

And then she went to a wooden box. Opening it, she took out a leather sheath and removed a hunting knife from it.

Handing it to him, she smiled.

"Paw'd be real pleased to know I give it ta someone in need."

Chase was touched by her generosity.

"Thank you, Oma. You're a good person."

He awkwardly grabbed her and hugged her, feeling the tenseness in her body at the new experience of being embraced. When he looked into her eyes, he saw tears. She turned to wipe her nose on the sleeve of her shirt.

Feeling refreshed both in his spirit and for his journey, he turned as he left the clearing to wave one last time to the generous soul who waved in return.

"Follow the crick fer 'bout a mile er two," she called after him.

And Chase Stewart was once again on his way to find Samantha.

11

A Virginia Battlefield
1864

Nathan

Union troops had been steadily moving south and pushing back the confederate armies. But the southern boys were up early this particular morning and union soldiers were taken by surprise. Nathan still had some breakfast in his hand when the first shots rang out. Somehow the rebels had gotten closer to them than was thought possible. The first volleys had taken down three union soldiers. Chaos broke out in the union camp. Soldiers scurried for weapons, every man shouting orders while the general mounted his horse to lead and sergeants frantically tried to organize their men.

But it was too late for some.

Nathan grabbed his rifle and some ammunition and headed for the protection of some nearby brush. Johnny Wills and Red Watkins came sliding in right on his heels.

"You see where they came from?" Red asked.

"Nope. All I know is soldiers started screamin' and runnin'," Johnny replied, quickly loading his gun as his eyes scoured their surroundings.

Funny how some things seemed to become second nature under pressure.

"Look out! On your left," Johnny shouted.

Nathan met Johnny Wills the first week he enlisted and they were good friends right from the start, possibly because they shared similar backgrounds. At any rate, they hit it off right away. Red

Watkins had joined the twosome a few weeks later and the three had become inseparable, boosting each other through the tough times with their jokes and good-natured pranks.

You could tell Johnny was proud of his military family by the way his blue eyes sparkled when he talked about them. His father was a commissioned officer; and when he talked about his mother, she sounded a lot like Nathan's own mother. Johnny often referred to himself as the black sheep of the family as his brothers as well as their father were all officers in the army. Johnny was capable…had the ability, but being in military command was not anything he relished. Sometimes Nate saw some of the same spirit in Johnny as he'd seen in his friend Chase Stewart.

Red got his nickname from his flaming red hair. There wouldn't be any officers or war heroes in Red's family. His father had been a drunkard and Red had basically supported his mother and little sister for most of his life. But Red had an open heart and loved a good joke, a quality that brought a bit of laughter to the troops. He took pride in his strength and was built like a cannon…muscular through the shoulders and solid as a rock. At least he had been at the beginning of this insanity. He, too, had lost weight during the process.

Mischief danced in his brown eyes when he was excited or plotting some mischief. Even his eyes seemed to have a splash of red in them.

"Whew! That was close!" Red panted as he reached the safety of the brush.

"Where are they and how did they get that close?" Johnny seemed irritated with the skill of the guards on watch.

"I don't know," Nate returned, "but they are here and too close for comfort."

At that point, Johnny's gun came to his shoulder and a deafening roar burst forth from the barrel. Nathan whirled around in time to see a confederate soldier take a couple steps backwards, grabbing for his chest. Turning to Johnny, he fought the wave of panic he felt.

"Thanks, man," he said solemnly.

"All a part of the job," Johnny replied as he struggled to reload. "Besides, ain't got time to baby you around if'n you get shot."

Red gave out with a burst of laughter.

"What you laughin' about?" Nathan growled. "It was probably your red hair that attracted them in the first place. Just like a red flag wavin' in the breeze. Gonna get you killed some day."

He touseled Red's mop of bright red hair.

Another shot whirred by their heads. All three assumed crouching positions while their eyes searched for the source.

"Put yer hat on," Nate yelled good naturedly at Red as the three prepared once more for another battle.

It was a long siege with dense smoke from the firearms and cannons and the deafening roar that blocked out any chance of hearing any orders. They just continued shooting and slowly the enemy fell and the bodies were strewn all across the land. Seeing signs of retreat, the boys held their ammunition and watched quietly from their vantage point. By the time they regrouped, orders had come down from the top that they were moving out. Grabbing their gear, the boys fell into line and the union troops marched farther south.

They had marched somewhere close to an hour when a scout came riding in fast.

"Ambush ahead," he yelled.

Orders to take cover were issued and men scattered as they sought protection from the attack. But it was too late for some who either hadn't reacted quickly enough through the confusion or hadn't comprehended the situation. As Nathan ran to the thickness of a grove of trees, he sensed bodies falling beside him but he kept running. Once secure, he loaded his gun and began firing. He was aware there were others with him doing the same thing. He had neither time nor presence of mind to discern if Red and Johnny were with him.

Faces smeared with dirt and gun powder and fear reflected the intensity of the attack. Suddenly from Nathan's left there came a rebel yell and two confederate soldiers broke the line and came in on top of them. Nathan remembered his gun leaving his hand with the impact of the first hit. Immediately he was wrestling with a soldier and fighting for his life as well. And this was a strong opponent and

Nathan found himself being pounded into the ground. He landed one good punch with his right hand and then a terrible pain covered the side of his head. He knew what he needed to do, but he couldn't get his body to respond. His breath was coming in short gasps and he realized there were strong hands around his throat. A fog descended over his eyes and brain as he looked into the face of his opponent. Suddenly the man's face disappeared and Nathan rolled to his side, attempting to once again fill his lungs with air. As he regained his breath, he began to stagger to get to his feet, heaving as he struggled. Blood oozed from his wounds and trickled down his cheek.

Nathan was on all fours when the man's face once again came into focus. Red held him from behind and then suddenly the man's face contorted and he slumped.

Red grabbed Nathan; and with his strong arms, pulled him to his feet.

"Let's get out of here!" he shouted, half dragging Nathan along with him.

They ran, dodging or tripping over dead bodies. It was a long day after the rebels retreated...a long day of taking care of the wounded and the dead.

Nate's head ached and fresh blood dripped down his face, but he was alive and walking and the union troops were on the move again. Red walked on one side of him and Johnny on the other to steady him when he felt faint. By the time a halt was called and camp was set up, he was exhausted.

"Better eat something," Johnny encouraged, shoving a tin plate into Nate's hand.

Nate's stomach convulsed with the smell of rancid food. He shoveled some of it into his mouth and then lay back on his bedroll, too tired to continue. He slept fitfully, his body fighting pain and his mind filled with images of Samantha and a beautiful summer day on the lake.

"Come on, Samantha," Nathan coaxed. *"It's such a splendid day."*

"I should be getting back. Mama will be worried about me."

"Can't you stay a little longer? We can go for a ride on the water," he pleaded.

She paused as if she were really weighing the consequences when all along she had intended to spend more time with him. Nathan was so much fun to be with and she loved hearing the stories he told. Mostly he would get her entire attention on some serious tale and then end with a rousing surprise. And each time she was taken in by his charm.

"Okay, I'll go, but you'd better be good at this rowing thing," she teased.

He helped her into the boat and followed her, pushing off from the shore as he did so. Taking the oars in his strong arms, he began to skillfully row them to the middle of the lake.

"You don't have to grasp the side of the boat so hard," he laughed.

"Only if I want to survive, she protested. *"Are you sure you've ever done this before?"*

"Once," he laughed. *"My Dad just pushed me away from shore when I was ten and told me to get back the best way I could. Guess I had to learn to row or be stuck out in the middle of the lake the rest of my life."*

"Nathan Clevenger, you just made that up," she scolded.

"Nope. Honest truth."

"Nathan, I can never tell when you're telling the truth or making up a story."

"Good," he exclaimed. *"That's just the way I want it."*

With that, he sent the boat in circles for a few spins.

Samantha knew he would never change. He would always have a story to tell that was near truth, but perhaps with a bit of fabrication. And she knew he did it just to amuse her. And she wouldn't have it any other way.

Nathan looked across the boat at Samantha, her dark hair gently blowing in the breeze, a blush of pink on her cheeks and with *that sparkle in her green eyes that told him how special he was to her.*

She had written to him. He still had the letter tucked away in his hip pocket. The pages were torn and ragged and stained, but he read the words almost every night. What was it she had asked? She invited him to come visit and told him that Hummingbird Hill was most beautiful when the magnolias were in bloom. With the image of Samantha Stewart in his head, Nathan sought a much deserved night of sleep. The next thing he knew, Johnny was waking him and the troops were ready to move out again.

12

Hummingbird Hill
Summer of 1864

Samantha

It was too hot to be out inspecting the cotton fields, but nevertheless it had to be done. And with Grady off to the war and Hardy missing for the second week in a row, Samantha had shouldered responsibility. She had learned what to look for . . . the hazards that needed to be dealt with and the signs of a good crop. This year's crop looked good; but with the war dragging on, would there be problems getting the product to market? And there was always the possibility of insect damage or drought. The darkies had continued to work despite the fact the overseer was missing, and that was a huge help and a welcome surprise in the face of the fact that the carrot of freedom was being dangled in front of them. But this was an exceptionally warm June and Samantha had lightened their load some throughout the middle of the day because of the heat...something she was quite sure would not meet with Grady's approval.

News from the war was slow in reaching York County. She had received only a handful of letters from Grady since his departure over two years ago...all during the first year...and had no idea if her letters were reaching him. And did she care? She found them difficult to write, not sure of what she was feeling. Mostly they dealt with the workings of the plantation, hoping she did not write anything that would cause him to worry or be concerned. Indeed, Samantha had learned to get along very well without Grady's help.

Life in South Carolina had taken on an entirely different atmosphere since the war had started.

News of the abolition of slavery had spread like wildfire among the plantations and many plantation owners were having difficulty with rebellion. Samantha felt comfortable that her slaves had chosen to remain on the plantation so far. Clover was the only one who showed any signs of rebellion. As a matter of fact, Samantha had even thought about selling her on the slave market before there were no more slave markets. And could she possibly do that? Sell another human being? As Grady would say, it was a question of economics and Clover would be prize material considering she had produced five offspring...four of them male...and was extremely healthy and a hard worker. Well, that could be dealt with later. Right now Samantha needed a break from the tedium of day to day work.

Satisfied there was nothing more to be done concerning the cotton fields, she pulled the wide brimmed straw hat tighter on her head, letting the ribbon tie fly into the wind and turned the big roan towards the high country.

There was one particular parcel of land Samantha was partial to. There were fruit trees growing there and a lush meadow filled with wildflowers; and a creek ran through it just begging one to slip off their shoes and wade in its cool waters. And it was Samantha's. The first year they were married, Grady had asked her what she wanted for her birthday, and that piece of property had been her request. It was a five acre tract of land and it was all hers. Although Mr. Hall, Grady's attorney, was shocked at the request, seeing as how women were not considered property owners at that time in South Carolina, it had been done. It was just as beautiful today as it had been the first time she saw it.

Turning the roan to the ridge, she continued her ride. From the ridge, she watched the confederate army transporting supplies at Nation's Ford across the Catawba. Nation's Ford was a natural ford in the river and had been used in years past by the Catawba Indians. Now a railroad bridge regularly supported trains carrying goods for the army of the confederacy and was a prime target area for union troops. Loss of the trestle would deprive the confederate army of a vital link in its supply line. Whichever side was in control of the trestle would be the side to control the war, at least in this part of South Carolina. It was the closest she had come to the actual workings of the war and it made her uncomfortable.

She felt for the pistol in the folds of her dress...something she never left the house without these days. Fortunately, she had not found a use for it. But it was a comfort to her to have it nearby. She smiled as she recalled Nathan allowing her to shoot a firearm. Little did she realize in those days of growing up that she might actually need those skills at this point in her life.

As she scrutinized the activity, she thought what a challenge it would have been for the threesome...Chase, Nathan and her...to have been a part of the proceedings she saw going on below her. Intrigue. Excitement. Adventure. That all seemed a lifetime ago.

Chase. The Stewart son named for his mother's family. How she missed her brother and his gentle smile and zest for life, the long talks they shared late at night. Lately, she felt a real connection to him, a strong pull as if he were trying to tell her something. She tried to shake that feeling. Maybe Father had permitted him to join the union forces. If so, where was he and was he safe? She shuddered to think he might be in danger. And mail, as infrequent as it had been, had been even less with the ongoing war. Waves of homesickness washed over her.

Clinton. No one could ask for a better older brother, always the level headed one, the one to sit her down and logically discuss her problems with her. He was considering marriage when she left with Grady to move to Hummingbird Hill and now she wondered if Clinton's plans had indeed materialized.

Edward. Such a ladies' man! No doubt he was still unattached but still available to all the young women in that part of Washington. And didn't she feel elegant when she walked down the city streets with the dashing Edward? She had gotten used to the fact that young women tried to get close to her in order to get close to Edward. He was suave and so good looking! Wondering how the war had affected his business, she somehow knew Edward was clever enough to survive.

Father. Samantha had been his special little girl. Spoiled? Maybe a little. Yet he had taught her to pursue education and be strong, to use her knowledge as well as her beauty; and she was drawing upon that strength right now with the managing of the plantation.

Mother. If she missed Father's guidance in matters of business, she missed Mother's wise guidance in life and domestic things. She fingered the locket she wore around her neck. It had belonged to Claudia Chase Stewart and Samantha's grandmother Chase, before her. Yes, Samantha missed her family.

But it wasn't only family Samantha missed.

Nathan. Friends since childhood. More than friends? It could have been. Even in all her happiness at the wedding, the sight of Nathan standing at the edge of the crowd of guests sent a shiver of sadness through her. She wanted to reach out to him then as she did now. Yes, Nathan had been on her mind as well. Chase had written that Nathan had enlisted in the war. Was he safe? His name had found its way into her prayers along with those of her family members.

Prayers fell short when she thought of Grady.

But the cares of everyday routine on the plantation called to her and she needed to get back to reality.

On her way back to the plantation house, she saw a figure running towards her. Izzy? That could only mean one thing…there was trouble at Hummingbird Hill. She spurred the roan into a gallop, pulling him up short in front of Izzy.

"What is it, Izzy?" she questioned. "What has happened?"

"Oh, missus Samantha," Izzy said, gasping for breath. "Youz gotta come quick. Mistuh Hardy iz back and he iz mean."

Samantha surveyed the scene as the roan's hooves beat a pathway to the plantation yard. It was as Izzy had said. A staggering drunken Hardy was standing in the middle of the yard, wielding the infamous whip in his hand. A figure cowered on the ground in the wake of his wrath. Samantha heard the whistle of the whip as it cracked through the air and then the thud as it landed on bare skin. The roan snorted as Samantha pulled him to a halt and slid from the saddle.

"What's going on here?" she demanded.

Hardy turned with evil in his eyes and raised the whip high over his head as if to strike out at a new target.

"I'd think twice about that," Samantha said firmly as a feeling of terror made its way up her spine.

He paused, looking at her through bleary eyes.

"Put it down, Hardy," she demanded.

He stared at her, his eyes ablaze with liquor.

"Put it down...now!"

"You ain't my boss," he slurred.

She felt panic as she feared that indeed he would not respond to her demands, but she mustered as much courage as she could.

"That's where you're wrong, Hardy," she said calmly. "I *am* your boss. And I want to help you. Now put down the whip."

He threw his head back and laughed, still holding on securely to the weapon.

"You ain't nothin' but a woman. Whut do ya think you can do to me?"

Samantha became aware of the fact that the entire slave population was watching the proceedings with interest either from the yard itself or from the doorways and windows of the slave cabins. Still crouched on the ground was Moses, the oldest of Callie and Elijah's children, blood spurting from fresh wounds on his back.

Reaching for the pistol in the folds of her skirt, she stepped forward towards Hardy and leveled the gun at him.

"Want to try to find out how much woman I am?" she said coldly. "Now drop the whip or prepare to be shot."

It was Hardy's turn to feel terror climb his spine. He suddenly became very sober, realizing that indeed Samantha was very much in control, and let the whip slip from his hands to the ground.

Keeping the gun still aimed at him, Samantha gave further orders.

"Go wash up at the well," she said. "Then come up to the porch. Hummingbird Hill will no longer be in need of your services."

Even though she realized that firing Hardy would present an entirely new set of problems, she paid him what was due him and sent him on his way. As she watched as he rode out the lane, she hoped that would be the last she would ever see of him. Then she found the comfort of her room and shook with emotion and tears. It was not an easy task to be mistress of a plantation.

The darkies went about their daily chores and Elijah and Callie bathed Moses' wounds with their usual home remedies.

"She be a strong woman," Callie said to Elijah as she worked tending to their son.

"Thet she iz," Elijah replied.

"She be fair," Callie continued.

"Yep, she be fair."

"Whut's botherin' you?" his wife asked.

"I'z pray she be safe," Elijah answered. "Strong wimmins haz it difficult sometime."

13

October, 1864

Clover

She ran as swiftly as bare feet could take her under cover of night, making remarkably little noise as she did. The padding of her bare feet against the ground made no more sound than her breathing. Although the evening air had started to cool, her thin gray dress clung to her body with perspiration. Her black eyes searched the darkness for any sign of movement. Mournful notes of slave songs from back at the cabins floated through the night air and reminded her of the constant danger she was facing. Her body was seasoned to hard work and her strong legs transported her quickly over the leaves that had begun to fall. Her destination? She wasn't sure. Mr. Tapp had always been able to find her once she was past the tree line that hid Hummingbird Hill from the river. It seemed he just suddenly appeared, as if he had been watching her since she'd left the plantation. As skilled as Clover was at knowing the territory, at seeing in the dark, he still always surprised her by his presence. It was a skill Clover needed to master as well.

Old Marsh had told her of the danger she would experience if she got involved. Old Marsh had been helping slaves move into northern territory for many years now and had been rewarded handsomely for information he furnished the north during the conflict. But there were places an aging dark man could go and there were places Clover could go where Old Marsh could not.

Clover, although born a slave and had been a slave all her life, was not content to stay a slave. She'd heard about freedom. She'd heard about a different kind of life; and although she could only dare to dream in the far reaches of her mind, freedom was something she coveted, especially since Massah Grady had gone off to the war. He said he would return, but she had no assurance of that from all reports she'd heard. So she was confident in the decision she'd made to obtain information for Mr. Tapp.

Her life at the plantation had not been horrible. Never once had she had the whip laid to her. There was always enough food. She adored Massah Grady and missed him terribly. While other slave women resented him, she enjoyed him and he enjoyed her. No other darkie on the plantation had rewarded him with four fine sons. That in itself had earned her a position above the other slaves...at least it had in her mind. No wonder she was special to him. In her eyes, having his children was the greatest accomplishment she could possibly have.

Clover's skin was ebony in color, the color of coffee that had been brewed too long. In contrast, Izzy's skin was lighter and shone like burnished copper in the sunlight. Clover would like for her skin to be that color, but Clover was strong and muscular and could work long hours in the massah's house without tiring. And having his babies was an easy task for her. And Ms. Samantha had been there two whole years before the war and had never given him a boy child.

There wasn't anyone on the plantation who questioned her place of importance; that is until that Yankee woman came to live there. That had changed everything. Well, almost everything. Dislike between the two women was instant. But massah said everything would be alright and nothing would change for Clover. And hadn't she seen the look on Ms. Samantha's face that day when Samantha saw the massah and Clover coming from the barn before he left for the war? That showed everyone how important Clover was.

The war! She'd heard there would be no more slavery after the war, that all slaves would be freed. And the day Old Marsh told her about becoming part of the spy network was the beginning of her real passion for attainable freedom. Clover had heard all about freedom and she intended to get her some. And meeting this officer of the union army tonight would help her achieve that freedom. No more working in the plantation house; no more taking orders from someone else.

She had already proved her loyalty by furnishing the union with valuable information on the movement of troops in the area; and since her facts had been substantiated, her credibility was established. Clover didn't really understand everything about the war, certainly not its ramifications or significance; but she was skillful in obtaining information.

"Over here," the voice whispered from the shadows.

Clover stopped and turned, amazed she hadn't seen him because his outline blended in so well with the trees. His stocky form came into focus and Clover approached the silhouette.

"Do you have information?" he asked when she neared.

"Ah do. The shipment iz gonna cum through on Sataday next," she told him.

"Are you sure?" he questioned.

"Ah'z positive," she responded.

"How many?"

"They's two carloads full an' twelve soldiers."

"Good work. What time?"

"They's cummin' late in the evenin' so's ya'all thinks they iz not cummin' on thet day, Mr. Tapp, suh."

He grabbed her arm.

"Ssh! I've told you never to say my name out loud."

"Yessir! Ah'z sorry, suh," she apologized.

Seizing her hand, he pressed something in the palm and she felt the smooth coolness of a coin. A bribe? For certain. She already knew too much. Why had he been careless enough to tell her his name?

"Thank you. We'll meet again the same time next week."

"Yessuh," she responded.

"Again, good work, Clover."

Then Mr. Tapp disappeared just as quickly as he had appeared.

Clover started back to the plantation, carrying the coin securely in her hand. It would be added to three others in her secret hiding place in the slave cabins.

The flame on the candle flickered in the October breeze from the open window in Samantha's bedroom. Blowing the flame to extinguish it, she walked to the window to close it for the night. As she overlooked the side yard, she saw the figure of a woman running towards the cabins. Was that Clover? It certainly looked like her. What in the world was Clover doing out at this time of night?

14

———————— ❦ ————————

Battlefield,
Late November, 1864

Nathan

A wet chill...the first of the winter...and an unexpected light snowfall only added to the misery of the encampment. The day had been spent trying to regroup after a sneak attack by the goober grabbers, as the confederate boys were not so affectionately called. Many among Nathan's regiment had been wounded, many were sick from malnourishment and unsanitary conditions. It was no consolation to know that the enemy camps fared the same if not worse.

Nathan made an effort to swallow the bully soup, a kind of gruel made of cornmeal and crackers mashed in boiling water spiced with ginger and wine. The cook, otherwise known as the Dog Grabber, had once again managed to concoct something almost edible. Nathan guessed the ginger and the wine were the key ingredients that made it palatable. And this unit was fortunate to have a cook rather than depending on their own resources. As usual, Nate sat huddled with Johnny Wills and Red Watkins, all pulling their blankets close around them as the chilled air threatened to seep into their bodies.

Moans of the sick penetrated the air along with the screams of those being treated and the groans of the dying.

"There'll be plenty of work today," Red said solemnly as he stopped eating with his spoon in midair.

"Yep," Johnny remarked.

"Gruesome work," Nathan muttered.

The words were no more than out of his mouth when Nathan threw his spoon against the tin cup and got to his feet in agitation.

"I can't eat listening to this," he barked.

"Sit down, Nate," Johnny said calmly. "Ain't nothing you can do about it. But you can keep yerself from getting down. Eat. You need it to survive."

Nathan continued to pace in frustration and then realized that Johnny was probably right. He'd been trying for more than two years now to fix this mess and the only thing he knew for sure was the fighting would continue and the dying was inevitable.

He sat back down and picked up the tin cup and continued to shovel down the soup.

"Hey, you there," the Sargent ordered. "Clevenger, Wills, Watkins. Over here. Help with these wounded."

The three of them moved, not out of respect for the order, but out of respect for the injured. It seemed like hours passed before they finished. One by one, they lifted the wounded to the surgeon's table; and one by one, they lifted them from it, many of them now without limb or life. The screams of those living out the torture were unbelievable and haunted them, stayed with them, never leaving them. Mini balls left wounds that were difficult to treat. Medical supplies were almost nonexistent.

Useless arms and legs lay in a pile near the surgeon's table like parts of a butchered beef. What small amounts of opium and morphine they had in their possession in no way covered the amount needed.

Sometimes Nathan and Johnny and Red held down the bodies of the injured as they lay on the table, helpless in the hands of a man who had little training and not much skill. Blood from one man on the surgical instruments blended with the blood from the next. The threesome tried to offer little bits of encouragement and Nathan even heard Red say a short prayer over those who had no chance of recovery. But there was no time to mourn. Those who felt the surgeon's knife had to be attended and those who didn't make it had to be buried.

And with that horrendous task finished, bodies were beyond tired. Maybe that's the way it should be…too tired to feel anything but the need for sleep. Perhaps that was the only way to cope with reality.

"Prisoners comin' in," came the word passed through the ranks.

It didn't happen often, but occasionally Nathan's outfit captured a few of the southern boys. Most had been handed over to bigger more influential units. However, it was always of interest; and every soldier's attention was directed towards the three prisoners who staggered into camp. Nightfall was approaching and their faces could barely be distinguished in the light from the small fires that attempted to keep the troops warm.

"Over here," directed one soldier and the group of three, with hands tied behind their backs, stumbled forward on command.

From his place nearby, Nathan could see that one was an older man...the one who walked with a limp...had graying hair at his temples and Nathan paused to wonder if the man had been old when he entered the conflict or if he had aged that much during the war. The second man was a sturdy fellow appearing to be several years older than Nathan. His long brown hair fell to the shoulders of his confederate jacket, the only uniform in the trio. Both men were unshaven. The third prisoner was just a young boy who was visibly scared and probably should have been at home taking care of his mother.

From the conversation that ensued, Nathan perceived the prisoners would be kept in their company only overnight. By morning an armed guard would come by and take them to a prison compound where they would be held for questioning...or whatever was done at those places. At least that's what Nate believed would happen.

Prisoners were usually sullen and kept to themselves; but the tallest of the three, the one in the confederate jacket, seemed to want to engage in conversation.

"What are your plans, suh?" he asked of the lieutenant as the lieutenant checked the prisoners' restraints.

Obviously annoyed with the prisoner, the lieutenant turned sharply.

"No concern of yours," was the reply. "Let's just say you should enjoy the comfort of this camp tonight. Tomorrow might not be as healthy for you."

The prisoner would not let it go.

"Is that a threat, soldier?" he questioned in his best southern drawl.

"Insubordination will not be in your favor, Mr...Mr..."

"Reynolds is the name, suh. It's a name ya'all shall not forget. Ah come from a long line of fahn southern gentlemen."

Such a defiant attitude certainly had the lieutenant's attention.

"Really?" the lieutenant quizzed. "You one of them plantation owners?"

The lieutenant's eyes narrowed as he came close to Reynolds' face.

"Why, yes suh, I am. A fahn one at that," Reynolds answered.

Normally the lieutenant would not even have a conversation with a prisoner, but he did not take kindly to arrogant men, let alone arrogant confederate men and the soldier's remark stirred an anger in him.

"Well, is it true what they say about the masters of the plantation?" the lieutenant's eyes narrowed. "You have your way with the black wenches anytime you want?"

Reynolds laughed a raucous laugh.

"It's two fold, my good man," he explained but did not deny its truth. "It keeps the females under submission and it increases the slave population at the same time."

Nathan could feel the anger rise in the lieutenant's voice.

"How does a southern lady feel about that? I assume you have one of those."

And at that moment, the lieutenant almost felt sorry for any woman who had been involved with such a self-righteous man.

"Suh, ya'll don't understand our ways. Our women understand. They've been brought up on the plantation. It's only those Yankee women who don't understand. Like the one ah married and brought down from the north. Huge mistake. Yeah, one of you Yankees. Have regretted it ever since."

Scorn could be heard in Reynolds' voice in his reference to Yankees.

Nathan's ears pricked up at that bit of information. He moved closer to the conversation. It was difficult to distinguish features of the man named Reynolds by firelight and the addition of a beard and mustache further clouded the picture Nathan had in his mind. Could it be? Was that even a remote possibility out of all the men in this war, this one should end up in this particular camp?

Apparently Reynolds didn't know when to stop talking. He continued his ranting and derailing the female gender.

"She doesn't understand either. You northerners surely understand that women are made for the pleasure of man. They're not good for much of anything else. If they can't satisfy their husbands they're not much use. Certainly not smart enough to be in the business world."

The lieutenant, with all his pride in his northern country welling up inside him and confronted by the insolence of this egotistical man in front of him, continued to ask questions. Nathan edged up beside him and whispered in low tones.

"Ask him his wife's name."

Although taken aback by the request, the lieutenant asked for the information.

With a toss of his head, Reynolds spoke loudly and coarsely, using some swear words as he did.

"You'all will not get that information from me," he jeered. "Just take it from me, she is a woman who looks like a beauty but is a devil instead with notions and ideas no woman should never have."

"Sir, you are not a gentleman in any sense of the word. I truly hope you are not a representative of all southern men."

The questioning was over for the evening. As Nate hunkered down between his buddies, his mind kept replaying what he'd heard. Was this the same man who had swept his beloved Samantha away from her family? Away from him? This man was crude and haughty and a braggart and undoubtedly deserved whatever torture might be in store for him. How could Grady Reynolds have exposed his intelligent, beautiful friend to such a life? And what had this beast of a man done to his sweet Samantha?

Nate slept fitfully, his dreams filled with images of Samantha being mistreated in a world strange to her. He woke early the next morning; and creeping close to the prisoners, he called out in a loud voice.

"Grady Reynolds, is that you?"

Grady immediately startled; and in his sleepiness, he responded to his name. So this indeed was the Grady Reynolds who had taken Nathan's beloved Samantha. Overcome with emotion, Nathan flew into a rage, attacking Grady with every bit of energy he had, pounding his face over and over again. When the rest of the camp realized there was a fight going on, they quickly roused. It took two of Nathan's fellow soldiers to restrain him.

"What's got into you?" Johnny demanded.

"Dirty, rotten goober grabber!" Nathan answered.

"We've captured others. Why did you let this particular one get to you?"

Nathan paced back and forth, rubbing his forehead with his hand and shaking his head.

"That's the ingrate who took Samantha from me and her family," he blurted out. "Why, oh why?"

Seeing he was clearly distraught, Red and Johnny attempted to console him.

"Didn't you hear all the things he was saying? How he disrespects women? And Samantha, *my* Samantha, was the brunt of his arrogance? It's more than I can think about."

"Let me at him," Red offered. "I'll take care of him once and for all."

And Nathan knew Red would do such a thing if only Nathan consented.

"No need," Johnny said, nodding in the direction of the prisoners. "The detail is here to take them away."

15

Late Winter of 1865

Chase

"Come quick, Pa," the ten year old yelled as he waded through the freshly fallen snow in the upper elevations of North Carolina's mountains.

Bending down over the still form of a young man, the boy quickly began to check for signs of life.

"Is he daid, Pa?" he asked of the older man who by this time had caught up with his young son.

Pa knelt down and intensely studied the figure crumpled on the cold ground. Removing the frozen blanket from around the man, he began to gently massage the man's arms and legs to stimulate circulation.

"Not yet," he finally said, getting to his feet. "But it won't be long if we don't act quickly. Git some evergreen branches...and, Rob...hurry!"

Rob was swift in his work and gathered plenty of evergreen branches to lay on the frame Pa was making of limbs he cut for poles. In short time, they had made a crude litter, but one that would get the job done, and had the unresponsive body strapped in.

"No time to waste," Pa said to the boy. "We need to hurry."

Rob tucked the gun under one arm and grabbed the hunting knives while Pa situated himself between the poles, dragging the litter after him. Rob had to run to keep up. Pa was a hearty man and strong and surely had to be exhausted by the time the cabin was in sight. But Rob knew Pa would not falter with a man's life in the balance. He sprinted ahead to open the cabin door and be ready to help get the frozen man inside.

"Build up the fire," Pa ordered.

Rob was glad he had carried in plenty of wood for the fireplace earlier in the day. That was one of his morning chores, and sometimes an evening chore if the weather turned bitter. And sometimes that happened in these higher elevations. Moving the soup kettle over the fire to heat, he hurried to gather blankets.

"Good boy," Pa said, proud to see his son was thinking and knew what to do.

Once again, Pa checked the body for signs of life, rubbing his extremities and placing quilts Rob handed him over the body. Rob was good help. Pa felt proud of his young son.

Chase lay still. His face was pale and frost still clung to his hair and clothing. He was so cold...miserably cold, life threatening cold...and all he wanted to do was sleep.

His mind floated with random dreams of earlier days.

"Chase, bring my little girl back to me," Claudia Stewart pleaded.

"I will, Mama," Chase promised. "You just try to rest and feel better."

Claudia's slender body rested comfortably in the crisp white sheets. Secretly, Chase hoped there would be enough time to make the journey and return.

"Hurry, Chase," she continued, reaching for his hand "You are our hope."

Chase swallowed hard as he took his mother's tiny hand in his.

"You can count on me, Mother. Now please rest and feel better. You need to be strong when Samantha comes home."

"Come on, little brother."

"Wait up, Edward," the younger Chase panted.

"But we're almost to the top, Chase. You can do it. Just think of the view once we get there. It'll be worth it. Come on, Chase. Try harder. You can make it."

"I'll race you to Monument Park," Nathan challenged.

"What are the stakes?" Chase was interested.

"Well, let's make it interesting," Nathan loved the sport.

"How much?"

Nathan thought a bit.

"Loser treats the winner to dinner at the Beef and Ale."

"You're on," Chase crouched over his horse. "And be sure to bring plenty of coin. You're going to need it."

As the boys raced, Chase could feel the cold breeze biting into his flesh as they flew past the cobbler's shop and the town hall and King's church. Nathan pulled ahead of him a bit and Chase urged his horse faster until they were neck and neck once again. Then he pulled ahead. But it was short-lived as Nathan once again took the lead. Mud flew from their horses' hooves and the wind from their speed pushed their hair and hats back on their heads.

As the two raced on, it appeared that neither could outdo the other. It would be a matter of whoever was ahead by the time they reached Monument Park.

The cold was bitter and Chase could feel the numbness in his hands as he grasped the reins.

Cold hands, cold face.

———————— ⁗⟨∕⟩⁗ ————————

"Chase. Chase, can you hear me?" Samantha asked.

She wasn't used to seeing Chase sick in bed, but the influenza was particularly bad this season. Wringing a fresh cloth, she applied it to his temples and tucked the blankets tightly around him. He moaned a bit in his fitful sleep.

"Think of the fun we'll have once the weather breaks," she continued to talk to the still figure. Laying her head against his chest, she continued to encourage him.

"You need to get better. Can you hear me? Can you hear me, Chase? Come on, you can do it."

———————— ⁗⟨∕⟩⁗ ————————

Chase continued his dreams. The past continued to pull at him, but he was so cold and just wanted to sleep. So tired. So cold. And then he would drift again into fitful sleep.

Pa kept watch over him, knowing this would not be an easy trip for the young man stretched out before him.

"Is he union or rebel, Pa?" young Rob asked.

Pa was silent a few minutes before he replied.

"Don't make no difference," he said. "Merely a man who needs our help right now. His politics ain't important."

Rob shook his head in agreement, always amazed at his father's compassion for others. And he knew for a fact that if this was a Yankee or a Johnny Reb, it would make no difference to Pa.

Chase's sleep was fitful, full of anxiety and he thrashed often in the bed, sometimes mumbling or sometimes shouting out several words. It was about noon of the following day when the tremors started. It took both Pa and Rob to hold him down.

"Is he dyin'?" Rob asked, never having witnessed this kind of behavior before.

"Not yet," Pa replied. "Right now he's probably wishin' he would."

The shivers were followed by fever which caused him to hallucinate. At times his eyes opened but Pa knew he wasn't comprehending anything and continued to sit patiently at his side, catching bits of information Chase yelled out from time to time. Among the words he spoke most often was the name *Samantha* which Pa concluded was someone pretty special to him. Chase struggled as the fever raged inside him. And then the fever finally broke leaving Chase drenched in perspiration and weak.

"He gonna be okay?" Rob asked.

"I think he will be now," Pa answered, carefully wiping perspiration from Chase's face with a clean wet cloth. "I think he's 'bout ready to try some of that soup now."

By the time Rob returned with a tin of soup, Chase was awake and lucid.

"Wh...where am I?" his throat was thick.

"This here's the Rice cabin," Rob volunteered, relieved their guest was awake. "And this here's my Pa and I'm Rob."

"Pleased," was Chase's only response.

So weak, so tired.

"Here," Pa Rice encouraged. "Try some of this soup."

And Pa carefully spooned some liquid into Chase's mouth. Chase thought he felt the spoonful of soup travel the entire pathway into his stomach. How long since he'd eaten? He didn't remember. The second spoonful of soup tasted better than the first; and the next, even better. Chase was hungry. That was a good sign.

"Ease up a bit," Pa cautioned. "Let your body get used to it. My guess is you haven't eaten too regular."

Chase nodded and lay his head back on the pillow in exhaustion. Once again sleep overtook him, this time a more peaceful sleep.

Two days later, Pa Rice and Rob were preparing poultices for Chase's chest. Standing from his squatting position and putting his hands at the small of his back to relax the tension of the past few hours, Pa let a sigh escape his mouth.

"Aint' good, is it, Pa?"

Pa Rice shook his head.

"Ain't good."

Their conversation was interrupted by another coughing outburst from the patient. Indeed, Chase Stewart was a very sick young man.

Days following were filled with warm fires, elevating Chase's upper body, steam from kettles for the patient to inhale and regular doses of Pa Rice's own particular brand of whiskey. At best, Chase was too weak to stand and Rob and Pa took turns spooning first soup and then grits down him until he was able to tolerate more substantial food. No questions had been asked until Rob stopped spooning one day and let his inquisitiveness take over.

"You got a name?"

Chase smiled.

"Yep. Chase…Chase Stewart."

"Thet's a funny name," Rob said, pushing another spoonful of mush into Chase's mouth.

"And yours?" Chase inquired.

"Same as I told you that first night we brung you here."

Chase responded with warmth towards the boy's openness.

"I don't remember much about that."

"You wuz mighty sick. Ah found ya when Pa and me was out huntin'. Darn near froze ta death, ya wuz."

"Why'd you help me?"

Rob laid down the spoon as if he couldn't understand how anyone could ask a question that had such a simple answer.

"Pa says it ain't right to let yer fellow man suffer."

"Your Pa sounds like a smart man," Chase offered.

"None smarter," Rob replied with pride.

He continued spooning. Pa said that was the only way their patient would regain his strength. So, if Pa said it, it must be true.

"You union or Reb?" Rob wanted to know.

"Does it make a difference?" Chase asked.

"Pa says a man's politics don't make no difference when a man needs help."

"Then your Pa *is* indeed a smart man."

That seemed to satisfy Rob for the moment and he continued spooning food into Chase's mouth.

Days passed and Chase grew stronger. He ate more and slept a lot, but each day proved to be a step towards recovery. Simple tasks like feeding himself and washing his face left him weak and lethargic. The day he somewhat unsteadily got to his feet and walked across the room was a milestone. He also began to be aware of his surroundings. His recovery space was a one room cabin with a huge fireplace at one end. Benches sat next to a crude table and one lone rocking chair with a tattered quilt hanging from it hovered in one corner of the room. Pegs beside the door held outdoor clothing and an assortment of guns stood nearby. A few cooking utensils were perched on a shelf on the other side of the door. One item which seemed totally out of place in this cabin setting was a rather ornate wooden clock which hung on the far wall. Rob noticed Chase's interest.

"It belonged to my Ma," he explained.

Chase sensed the sadness in the boy.

"She died."

Chase put his hand on Rob's shoulder. Little boys shouldn't be without their mothers.

But Rob's melancholy was only for an instant or two. Chase could feel the determination and strength in this young man. Pa Rice had done a good job in raising this son.

Long winter nights were good for healing and conversation and for spinning tales. Chase had just finished an epic story about Samantha, Nathan and himself; and Rob was fascinated by the whole thing.

"It must be great to have family," he said.

Chase shot a quick look at Pa's saddened face.

"You have your Pa," Chase consoled.

"Oh, Pa and me do fine," Rob was quick to add. "But I still wonder what it would be like to have brothers and a sister like you...and a mother."

Chase saw the sadness that came into Pa's eyes, the sadness that comes from missing a loved one, the sadness of a Pa wanting to give his son more than he could offer.

"You got more than most," Chase continued. "There's a lot of kids who'd trade places with you in an instant to be living out here in this secluded place and hunting and fishing and living off the land with their Pa."

Pa nodded his head as he puffed away on his pipe. He approved of Chase's response and it seemed to have satisfied Rob.

Chase Stewart once again realized how lucky he was.

"Is she purty?" Rob asked as Chase and he split and brought in more wood for the fireplace. "Your sister, I mean."

"Oh, yes, she's really pretty with her dark hair and green eyes. And she's fun to be with. She and our friend, Nathan, and I...well, we managed to get into lots of trouble growing up. Nothing really bad, but mischievous."

"Ah don't know thet word. You sure use some fancy talkin'."

"Well, it means just a bit naughty, but nothing bad or mean," Chase tried to explain.

Rob was quiet for a few moments. Then he loaded his arms with firewood.

"You're gonna leave us soon, aren't you?" he said sadly.

"Yes, Samantha said to come when the magnolias are in bloom," Chase told him.

"Yeah, you talked about that a lot when you wuz sick."

Once again there was a silence between the two.

"They'll be in bloom in another couple of months," Rob said and Chase wondered at the wisdom this little boy possessed.

"Reckon it's time."

Chase saw the resolve in the young boy's demeanor.

"Yep," Rob said quietly. "Reckon it's time."

16

Battlefield,
Early Spring 1865

Nathan

War has its way of entwining itself into the senses...forgotten for a time, but relived for the rest of one's life, surfacing in ways and places one would never suspect. The smell of gun powder igniting, of body odor from too many days of uncleanliness, the dankness of early mornings, the rancid smell of rotting food, of human excrement, of decaying flesh, of wood fires burning in the campsite.

The rumble of the cannons as they're being hurriedly transported to more advantageous positions, the boom of the shot as the cannonball leaves the barrel and then the thud as it hits its target, the groans of the dying, the sounds of generals issuing orders, the calls to battle and retreat emitting from fife and drum and bugle, the chaotic sound as men hurry into battle and the deadly silence when the guns cease firing.

Then there's the haze produced by the firing, the fear in the faces of the brave, the relief in one's chest to see the standard bearer's flag still waving above the turmoil.

One can taste the gun powder in the air. It is no worse than the taste of contaminated rations. Sometimes one can even taste victory or defeat.

One can feel the heat, the cold, the anxiety, the hope, the despair, the sadness, the loneliness, the pain. And then sometimes one can stop feeling anything at all.

This then, is the reality of war.

It had been a good night. Sir Charles, as he was affectionately known, was in an exceptionally good mood. That could only mean one thing…there would be music in the camp tonight. Sir Charles would produce his mouth organ, which normally was tucked away in his cap or haversack along with other valuables, and would strike up a lively tune. That always lightened the mood of the boys. Soon a banjo would be added and a mouth harp or as it was better known, a juice harp or Jew's harp. And if Johnson's fiddle had survived the latest skirmish, perhaps there would be fiddle music.

Soon there was a lot of laughing and joking and Red, with the help of a little whiskey, began to dance around the fire. Before long, others joined him and some just looked on, enjoying the reprieve from the more serious side of their comrades. If the song was a familiar one that had words such as *Yankee Doodle, Dixie,* or *the Battle Hymn of the Republic*, several would join in with a rousing chorus or two. When the words were in question, soldiers frequently made up their own lyrics. Songs were continually being written during the war years; and if they were lucky enough to make it into the camps, they were welcomed.

Once in a while, if the two opposing armies were camped near each other, the musicians had somewhat of a contest, letting their music compete through the air.

Each soldier had his own set of memories as he listened to the strains of the melodies piercing the night air. Some were thinking of wives or sweethearts back home or thinking pleasant thoughts of the war finally coming to an end and perhaps returning to loved ones. Truly it was a relaxing evening and all the boys in the troop went to bed with a bit of lightheartedness for a change.

Nathan awakened from a dream about dancing with Samantha to the sound of horses' hooves. He wasn't the only one who had heard them. Most soldiers learned to be tuned into the sounds around them. It seemed to be one of the first lessons learned in the military. Men began to scramble and reach for their weapons.

"Wake up, Red," Nathan shouted as he shook his friend.

Red, feeling the effects of last evening, was still groggy from sleep.

"Hurry," Johnny encouraged. "We need to take cover."

The three found cover just in time for the invasion. Gunfire burst out all around them. Red immediately began loading guns for Johnny and Nathan so they could keep firing.

"Faster," Nathan cried.

"Can't go no faster," Red responded.

Johnny and Nathan continued changing off guns with Red for several minutes of hectic firing.

"Come on, Red, you're slowing up," Nathan yelled.

There was no response, at least none he could hear above the commotion.

"Hey, Red, keep 'em comin.' I think we got 'em on the run."

He flung his arm backwards to receive the next loaded gun, but none was there. Nathan turned to see Red lying in a pool of blood. He quickly crawled to him.

"No. Please, no," he shouted, taking Red's body into his arms and holding him close.

"Sorry, Nate," Red whispered.

"Don't talk," Nathan urged. "It's okay."

"My hat," Red was struggling now to speak.

"Yeah, you lost your bloomin' hat. That's why you got hit. They must've seen your red hair."

"Address…in…hat," Red murmured.

By that time, Johnny was by their side.

"Here's the hat," he said as he handed the well-worn cap to Nathan.

"I've got the hat, Red. And a piece of paper."

"Tell them…"

Red had spoken his last words.

Nathan grabbed him by the shoulders and shook him.

"No. No, you can't die! Not now! Not ever!" Nathan screamed.

Holding Red's still form in his arms, he sobbed into his red hair. Blood from Red's open wound covered the front of Nathan's jacket as Nathan rocked and crooned over the body.

Hours later, Johnny came and put a hand on Nathan's shoulder.

"He was the strongest of us all," Nathan said simply as he looked up at Johnny's grim expression, his face stained with the tears that had flowed freely.

Johnny nodded in agreement.

"I was only kidding him about his red hair," he said, looking at Johnny through swollen eyes.

"He knew that," Johnny consoled.

Johnny had brought others with him and they pried Nathan's arms from around Red's body and buried him while Nathan stood nearby clutching Red's cap and the piece of worn paper he'd carried throughout the entire war.

Susanna. 1402 Cambridge, Washington, D C.

Nathan knew Susanna was Red's little sister. He tucked the piece of paper in his own cap along with his other prized possessions, including Samantha's letter.

Nathan didn't speak to anyone for two days. Finally Johnny approached him.

"Come on, soldier. Let's win this war and get back home."

17

Hummingbird Hill,
April 1865

Samantha

Hardy crossed over the Catawba River on Thursday afternoon. On Friday he encountered union soldiers on the road. Hardy's allegiance was to himself, not either side in the war.

" 'Mornin', boys," he said, reining in his horse and stretching in the saddle to relieve his back from the ride. He thought putting his hand to his wide brimmed hat out of respect to the officer was a nice touch.

"Good morning, sir," the sergeant acknowledged.

"How can I be of service to you boys?" Hardy asked.

"Are you familiar with the territory?"

"I am," Hardy responded, feeling his own importance.

"We are in search of sustenance for our men. Do you know of any place where we are likely to find some food? Our men have been on the march for several days now and we are low on supplies. We thought perhaps there was a farm nearby where we could barter for some supplies."

Hardy saw his chance to get even or at least to cause some frustration for his recent firing as overseer at Hummingbird Hill. A smile curled at the corners of his mouth.

"As a matter of fact, ah do," he answered, relishing the opportunity to possibly repay Samantha Reynolds back for letting him go.

"After you cross the river, continue to bear to your right. There's a plantation with plenty of food for all your men. And it's run by a woman in the absence of her husband so she should give you no trouble. Take what you will. You can see the plantation from the bluff once you cross the river and head a bit west. A long line of trees on either side of the lane leads to the house itself. There's a sign…Hummingbird Hill…you'll recognize it. It's the only plantation around for several miles."

"Why, thank you, sir. We appreciate your good advice."

"Remember, the trestle is controlled by the rebs. They'll be watchin'."

"Thank you," the sergeant muttered.

Hardy noticed the glint in the corporal's eye at the thought of a confrontation with the enemy.

With a quick thank you, the soldiers continued on their way and Hardy waved after them; then chuckling to himself, he turned his horse and headed north. Samantha Reynolds would surely be surprised by her visitors.

The detail of five continued pressing forward. After watching the routine at the trestle from a distance, the sergeant decided to wait for the cover of night to cross upstream without being detected.

First rays of daylight were streaking across the eastern sky when the detail saw the magnificent plantation house.

"Wow, that's some fancy piece of property," the corporal said in his crudeness. "These southerners really know how to live!"

"Don't get any ideas, Barton," the sergeant warned.

"Aw, c'mon, let's have a little fun, Sarge," Barton said as he turned his head aside to spit tobacco juice. "Maybe just a souvenir or two. Don't think they'd miss it."

The sergeant didn't answer but spurred his horse forward.

Izzy was the first to spot the riders when they were still at the far end of the lane.

"Miz Samantha," she cried as she ran towards the house.

Samantha burst through the front doors.

"Goodness, gracious, Izzy, whatever is the matter?"

"Someone's comin'."

Samantha crossed the porch and made her way down the front steps.

Putting her hand over her eyes to shade them, Samantha squinted in the bright sun. Certainly figures of the riders were unfamiliar to her.

"Izzy, go get my pistol," she told her. "And hurry."

Izzy scurried to retrieve the gun while Samantha studied the approaching figures. Soldiers. No doubt. It was unusual for military of any kind to make an appearance at the plantation since the plantation was just out of the mainstream of any active part of the war.

Izzy arrived with the gun which Samantha took and held at her side, concealed in the folds of her dress skirt.

"You go run and tell Callie to gather the folk in the cabins," she ordered.

Izzy ran off to complete the assigned mission while Samantha concentrated on the unexpected visitors.

"Stop where you are," Samantha called out as the group of five approached.

The sergeant held up his hand and the men brought their horses to a halt.

"State your business," she demanded.

"We come in peace searching for food, ma'am. We do not wish any trouble."

"That's good to know," Samantha replied. "Trouble is not welcome here. But we don't have a lot of food ourselves. There are many mouths here to feed."

"Ma'am, I sense by your accent that you support our cause...that of the Yankee troops."

Samantha hesitated before she answered.

"Sir, it's true I come from the north, but now am in charge of running this plantation."

She paused.

"But I can offer you some food."

She turned and shouted across the yard, knowing full well many pairs of eyes were watching from the confines of the slave cabins, the fields and the yards.

"Moses, Aaron, please come here."

The union detail watched as two rather large darkies emerged from the gardens and came to Samantha's side.

"Please bring two hams and three geese from the smokehouse and a bag of potatoes from the cellar and all the freshly baked goods from the kitchen."

Moses and Aaron started off at a trot to fulfill her wishes while Samantha kept an eye on her visitors and the soldiers sat uneasily in their saddles.

"You can put the gun away, ma'am," the sergeant said.

"Sir, you run your army the way you wish. I will run this plantation in a manner in which I see fit."

Corporal Barton quickly attempted to cover up a laugh. He found this woman, this fiery woman, extremely interesting. And beautiful.

"How about some liquor? You got any of that?" he leered.

"Sir, it seems to me that someone of your disposition could not be further enhanced by the consumption of hard liquor. The fact is, it would probably bring out the worst in you, if that is indeed possible."

Others in the company laughed at Barton's expense.

"I guess she told you," one said.

Barton was taken aback by her brashness, but at the same time found it exciting.

"You sure got some fancy words," he addressed Samantha.

"That's enough, Barton," the sergeant warned.

Moses and Aaron arrived with the staples Samantha had asked for and Barton dismounted to receive the items. In doing so, he moved close to Samantha.

"You sure are one purty woman," he leered through missing teeth.

"Corporal," the sergeant reprimanded, "bring the supplies and let's be on our way."

With a thank you from the sergeant, they departed. It was only then that Samantha felt comfortable enough to relax her grip on the pistol.

"Izzy, tell Callie we need more baked goods," she said. "Oh, and tell John I need to see him."

Moses and Aaron returned to their work while Izzy hurried off to relay the message.

Izzy's John came in a hurry.

"John," Samantha said. "I do not trust those men who were just here. Keep an eye out in the fields and let me know if you see them...or anyone else you consider suspicious."

"Yes'm," John replied.

And Samantha knew she could trust John in the matter. Izzy's John was a good man.

Samantha stood for a long time watching the soldiers as they moved off and cut across to the Catawba. Several concerns surfaced in her mind. First, now the union troops knew where there was likely a supply of food. Secondly, they were aware that a woman was in charge of the plantation and therefore probably considered it vulnerable. And thirdly, Samantha was uneasy about the corporal's comments.

Supplies of food were short in the union camp as well as every other camp in this horrible war, but whiskey flowed freely. The food the detail had brought back from Hummingbird Hill was a welcome addition to their diet.

"You shoulda seen it," Barton was telling his fellow soldiers. "Big and fancy. Rich, I'll bet. You can tell those things, ya know. And the purtiest little gal you ever did see."

"Yeah, you jest been gone from civilization so long, you'd think a heifer cow was purty."

This brought a round of raucous laughter from the soldiers, but it didn't dissuade Barton from continuing.

"Nah, I'm not kiddin'. 'Bout so high, so big around and big green eyes."

The more whiskey he consumed, the rowdier he became and the more concentrated his thoughts were towards the owner of Hummingbird Hill plantation.

Three nights later, Barton's fantasy became reality as he urged his horse through the shallows of the Catawba and up its steep banks and across the land to the path that led to the plantation house and the woman who had been in his mind since he first saw her. Moonlight lit the way when it wasn't hidden behind a cloud or two which made his course easy to follow.

All was quiet as he approached the darkness of the house, having walked his horse the last quarter of a mile or so in order he not be detected. Only one thing had been on his mind since he left camp…the beautiful woman he had seen at the plantation. And she was spunky, too. Talked right up to him. He liked that in a woman. A little fire; a little excitement. And it had been a long time since he'd felt that kind of excitement. Too long.

Samantha was asleep in her upstairs bedroom. Having been restless since the union detail's visit, she kept the pistol next to her bed. Several times that night she had been awakened by the slightest sounds and had gone to the window to look out over the side yard. Once she had even crept down the stairs to check the first floor of the house. All seemed at peace under the cover of moonlight. Returning to bed and pulling the covers up around her, Samantha finally drifted into a deeper sleep.

Barton tried the front door of the plantation house. Locked. But he did find an open window. Carefully raising the sash and crawling through the open space, he entered the library. Using the light from the moon, he gazed in awe at the collection of precious items. His first thoughts were to remove some of the treasures from their resting places; but he was not here for that kind of treasure. Moving across the room to the double pocket doors that opened into the grand entrance hall, he found himself at the foot of the staircase to the second level. Step by step, he made his way cautiously up the first flight of stairs where the steps began to curve. After pausing for a deep breath and a look around, he then proceeded to mount the ten or so remaining steps.

She sat up in bed, a feeling coming over her of complete terror. Looking around the room, she saw nothing different than the last time she was awakened. But still there was this feeling, this uncomfortableness, this premonition that something was about to happen. Turning back the covers on the bed, she stood; and reaching for the pistol and checking the ammunition, she took a few steps.

What was that? Had she heard something? She listened. No further sound came. Creeping to the open window, she glanced once more to survey the cabins and the side yard, the stables, the cotton fields beyond them. Nothing. No sign of activity. Still, she could not get past the feeling. Then she heard the door knob on her bedroom door being turned and a tingling sensation seized the back of her neck.

Other rooms stood with their doors open and he had found them empty. Only this one remained closed. This, then, must be the lovely lady's room. Placing his hand on the door knob, he turned it slightly.

Samantha's breath came in short gasps; that is, when she breathed at all. She edged her way from the window to the security of the dressing screen which stood in one corner of the room.

She poised the gun ready for use as she saw the figure of a man walk cautiously towards her bed. It was at that moment the moon decided to disappear behind a cloud and her vision was obscured as was that of the intruder. She strained to see what he was doing. He strained to see the woman he thought was in the bed.

The one advantage Samantha had was that she knew the layout of the room. The man did not. He misjudged the distance from door to bed and stubbed his toe against the bedpost in the darkness of the room.

"Dang it," he said out loud.

That voice sounded familiar. But where had she heard it before?

Just then, the moon sailed past the cloud and lit the room once more.

Immediately, Samantha recognized Barton, the union corporal who had paid a visit to the plantation a few days earlier. Also taking advantage of the moonlight, Barton realized there was no one in the bed. He turned and Samantha felt she had no recourse but to confront him.

"Get out or I'll blast you where you stand," she demanded in the calmest voice she could muster.

Realizing what he had come for was standing right in front of him, he quickly gathered his wits.

"Sorry, ma'am, I didn't mean to scare you," he attempted to apologize. "A woman like you probably gets lonely without a man here."

Samantha shuddered as he began to walk towards her.

"I said," Samantha gritted her teeth, "get out of here! Right now!"

Before she could take aim, he rushed towards her, grabbing for the gun. Although he was unsuccessful in his attempt to get the weapon, he did manage to grab Samantha by the wrist. Not being totally unfamiliar with fighting thanks to spending hours with Nathan and brother Chase, she elbowed him with her free arm. The sound of his laughter made her fight all the harder.

Knowing swiftness was utmost, she stomped on his foot and scratched at his face which caused him to temporarily lose his grip. As he recovered, he grabbed her from behind. Still she was able to keep the gun from his reach, but that did not help her in breaking his hold. Digging her fingernails into one of his hands, she pried a finger of that hand loose and turned it back as far as she could. Jumping with pain, he momentarily lessened his grip and she was free again. She whirled around, pointing the pistol directly at him, but he knocked it from her hand and she heard it go skidding across the floor. When she turned in an attempt to find the gun that was on the floor, he was upon her, knocking her to the ground. For a moment she lost her breath completely with the impact. He pushed her face into the floorboards, causing her air supply to diminish and excruciating pain to sprint across her face. She attempted to crawl, but he was too heavy; so she stretched as far as she could with her right arm to try to reach the gun, but it was beyond her reach.

Her right arm was free. If only she could get a grip anywhere on his body! His breath was warm against her neck. That meant his head should be within her reach. Moving her free arm up over her own head, enduring the pain of the awkward position, she felt for his hair; and twisting her fingers as tight as she could around it, she pulled with all her might. At first she thought it wouldn't be enough to inflict sufficient pain and she felt his body retaliate by smashing her tighter against the floor. She thought her nose would break for sure and felt the stickiness of blood as it began to bleed freely, but she kept her grip on his hair and pulled as hard as she could.

When she felt his head move to one side, she edged her already numb fingers around to his face and felt for his eyes. When she thought she could, she released the hair and pushed against the eye socket as hard as she possibly could. It worked. He moved and she rolled free; and finding the pistol, she scrambled to her feet and pointed it at him. Still screaming with pain, he looked through his swelling eye and prepared to lunge at her. She pulled the trigger and his body fell at her feet, blood splattering over her face and clothing. Samantha heard the deafening roar from the gun and then heard nothing. Dropping the pistol, she collapsed to the floor.

As her ears began to adjust, she could tell that the gunshot had aroused the darkies and she wanted to go to the window to solicit help, but she lay exhausted on the floor. The rapid beat of her heart resounded in her own ears. Nausea threatened and sweat poured down her face. Finally the perspiration that covered her face and mixed with blood from her bleeding nose slowly began to dissipate. As she struggled to get to her feet, she heard footsteps coming up the stairs. John rushed to her side.

"Iz you alright, Miz Samantha?" he asked.

"Light the light, John," she responded. "Let me see what I've done."

"John, John! What haz happened?" Izzy called from the stairway.

John fumbled for the lamp. The scene was even eerier in the glow from the oil lamp. A disheveled Samantha stood in her torn nightclothes, the ones that were spattered with her blood and that of the intruder. And a man's body covered in blood lay on the floor.

Izzy was at the doorway now and covered her mouth as she comprehended the scene.

John rubbed his huge hands over his head.

"Miz Samantha done shot a man," he said simply. "She be protectin' the plantation."

Mid- May, 1865. In the last months of the war, Union General George Stoneman and union troops under his command made a sweep through the area burning and pillaging as they went.

Although his main centers of attack were focused on the destruction of iron works and mills in an effort to shut down the confederate army, nothing was spared. The south would be crushed once and for all.

"Miz Samantha, they is cumin'," Izzy said as she ran to the plantation house with little Hope in her arms.

"Who, Izzy?"

"The soldiers. John haz been watchin' 'em two days now and they iz on their way here."

Izzy was clearly distraught.

"We haz got ta get outta here! He sez no more than half an hour away."

Izzy sobbed as she screamed out the words.

Samantha flew into action. First she gathered ammunition and firearms and some money from the library desk as well as the ledgers. She sent Izzy to the kitchen to put as much food as she could into a pillow case. After that, it was grab what she could.

"John, tell the slaves to find shelter and protection where they can," she ordered.

"They's a cave up on the hill," Izzy suggested.

By that time, John was back with them. Taking Hope from Izzy's arms, he took off at a lope with the two women following behind, struggling to keep up with his long stride. His legs were long and strong and it was difficult for the two women to follow at any close distance. Samantha frequently looked behind her to see the scurry of activity as the slaves took shelter. She was aware that Elijah must have turned the stable horses loose. Then, as she looked beyond the house, she saw the colonnade of troops coming at a fast pace up the lane to the plantation.

"Hurry!" Izzy shouted.

There was no time to look back now. Samantha ran without turning although she heard the shouts of the soldiers and gunshots behind her as they pillaged the plantation.

She fell as she ran, quickly getting to her feet, ignoring her torn dress and the pain in her forearm. Panting, she found the safety of the cave and collapsed on the floor. Izzy sat beside her, cradling a crying Hope in her arms as she attempted to soothe her.

John stood at the entrance to the cave. They were far enough away that he couldn't make out what was going on for sure, but smoke was visible from the barn area.

Samantha joined him.

"Can you see anything?" she asked.

"Nothin', Miz Samantha," he lied. "Too far away."

John hurriedly took a knife he had found in his haste in the kitchen of the plantation house and cut and broke some branches from the backside of nearby trees. If anyone came looking, they would maybe not be able to see the fresh cuts. He dragged them in front of the cave opening so no one could see their footprints in the ground. Then he placed them at the entrance of the cave as a barrier to the opening. Only then was he able to join his family and Samantha inside. There was nothing else to be done for now but wait.

Samantha busied herself, concentrating on the task at hand, taking inventory of what they had been able to bring with them. Two blankets, the pistols with ammunition, some matches and a candle, a few articles of clothing. Izzy had done a good job with the food from the kitchen. There was some ham, biscuits, potatoes from the breakfast meal, some fried chicken from the evening meal the night before and a dozen or so fresh fritters made just that morning and a jug of milk as well as some apples and dried fruit.

Although they slept fitfully in the dampness of the cave, Samantha was wakened in the early morning hours by sounds coming from outside the cave. Creeping on her hands and knees, she looked through the barrier of tree branches and was grateful for John's knowledge in putting them there. She saw three men in union uniforms mounted on horses searching the area. At one point, they were so close to the entrance of the cave that she could see their horses' breath in the early morning chill.

Hope moaned in her sleep and Samantha was almost sure it was heard because one of the soldiers stopped and looked around. Samantha reached out to touch the little one's cheek. As much as Samantha hated how Hope was conceived, the tiny girl was sweet just like her mother and there was no doubt that Izzy loved her baby girl. Izzy was a good mother. Her skin was lighter in color than

Izzy's, but she had Izzy's wide brown eyes. Hope was both pleasant and adorable. Samantha could not help but care for the little girl.

Possibly the three union soldiers had not heard any unusual sounds; and apparently satisfied it was nothing, the three prepared to leave.

"Whut iz it?" John roused.

"Shh," Samantha cautioned as she crawled back to the blanket. "Union soldiers scouting the area."

They waited and then came the words.

"You two go on ahead," the soldier said. "I'm going to search a bit more."

Samantha held her breath and John's eyes grew wide in terror as they realized the threat of being found was eminent. As they listened, they heard the soldier return and dismount to examine the strewn branches a little bit closer. Samantha motioned for John to stand on one side of the entrance and she took the other. Sure enough the branches began to separate and the soldier's arms became visible. Samantha grabbed from one side and John from the other, forcing the man to the ground. The sound woke Izzy and she cradled Hope so she would not cry. John removed the rope he used as a belt and tied the man's wrists behind his back. Before he could utter a sound, a piece was torn from Samantha's dress and stuffed in the man's mouth. But now what? Surely the others would come looking if the soldier did not return.

Samantha pushed aside the branches and looked out. All was quiet and only the soldier's horse stood nearby grazing on succulent shrubs. Moving cautiously and whispering to the horse, she was able to approach him and take hold of its bridle and walk him into the cave. The branches were carefully put back in place. Now they had a union soldier and his horse in their hiding spot. What came next, no one could predict.

April also saw the end of another part of the war. That's when the explosion came. The railroad trestle over the Catawba River was no more. Although it had been protected by the Home Guard, no one actually knew what took place that evening...whether the union forces had successfully cut off the vital link of confederate supplies or whether the confederate boys had done it intentionally. At any rate, it was done. Samantha had kept an eye on the operation every day and had even seen the procession the day General Robert E. Lee had led troops across the waters of the Catawba.

"Hush," Clover cautioned from her hiding place.

Samuel broke off a piece of hoe cake and offered it to his little sister, Aseneth, to keep her quiet.

"They haz taken ev'rythin'," she gasped as she witnessed the ravaging of the plantation. "Everthing Massah Grady haz worked for."

Her sons sensed their mother's concern.

"Whut we gonna do?" Isaiah asked.

"It's time we find Old Marsh. He'll know whut ta do."

She watched for some time; and as the soldiers seemed to be satisfied with their work and dissipated, Clover knew it was time.

Yous stey close by me," she admonished. "We be leavin' now."

With that, Clover turned her back on the only way of life she'd ever known. Three coins jingled in the pocket of her dress and five children followed her into the night as they made their way far away from Hummingbird Hill.

18

*The Battlefield,
Mid-May*

Nathan

They heard the pounding of horse's hooves before they heard the voice yell out the words.

"It's over! It's over! Lee surrendered and the war is over!"

Although the news traveled slowly across the states, it was welcome news. After four long years of fighting and the loss of more lives than anyone dared to think about, the war of cessation had finally come to an end. It took several days for the word to reach Nathan's unit. The North had prevailed. But where was the celebration? Tired bodies, anxious to return to any kind of normalcy, reacted in many different ways. Some were whooping it up by drinking and being loud. Some sat quietly. Some cried. All experienced relief. It seemed incomprehensible.

The war was finally over. Fighting would stop. But now, what? The news, so long in coming, seemed unbelievable. It was difficult to know they would wake up the next morning; and instead of finding and engaging the enemy, they would start finding their way home. Home? What was that? Where was that? So many things had changed!

"What are you going to do?" Johnny asked.

"Guess I'll head north and work my way back to Washington, D.C. Part of me wants to go; part doesn't. I don't know what to expect when I get there. There haven't been any letters for such a long time. But I need to know what's happening there. How about you?"

"Home. Then I'm thinking about heading out to Dakota Territory. I need to put this war behind me. Maybe even go farther west. See some new land. Just pack up and ride off into the sunset. Wanna come?"

"Sounds good, but I need to check family first. And then I promised Red..." his voice trailed.

"Yeah. Find his little sister."

"It's the least I can do. Sure hate to leave him in this Godforsaken country."

Tears began to form in Nathan's eyes at the thought of his friend. Johnny put his hand on Nathan's shoulder.

"I know," he said softly.

As the two prepared to leave the encampment, evaluating what they needed to take with them, Nathan put the address for Red's sister and Samantha's soiled and worn letter and what food he could store into his haversack and cap. With good natured hugs and wishes for safe travel, he and Johnny parted ways and Nathan began the long road back.

The south was beautiful in the spring of the year...perhaps more noticeable this year than the past few springs. Somehow its freshness symbolized the beginning of a new start. Healing from the war would not come easily. It would continue to fester in the hearts and minds of some people for years to come. But just now, as Nathan started his trek towards home, although his belly rebelled from lack of food, he could feel nothing more than the thrill of freedom. Maybe the end of the war meant freedom from slavery for some; but for others, there was the freedom from the fighting and killing. That's what Nathan felt on this glorious spring day. In the quietness of the early morning, he would begin to heal from the inner wounds that haunted him.

Once in a while he encountered a confederate soldier headed in the opposite direction and they exchanged a few words. If Nathan wanted to stop and rest a bit, he did; if he wanted a nap, he took the time to nap. Even small animals seemed to feel secure enough to be out and about now the shooting had ceased; and streams seemed to have replenished their supply of fish. Three days out, he found a pleasant place near a good fishing spot and caught three fish which he cleaned and cooked over a small fire he had built for just that purpose. The aroma of the frying fish filled the air and Nathan's stomach looked forward to the treat when he heard the noise. Leaving his fish, he pulled his gun and headed towards the sound. Upon coming closer, he saw a young man probably a few years younger than himself, sitting, rocking back and forth as he huddled with his arms around his legs, tears streaming from his face.

"What's going on here?" Nathan cautiously inquired.

The young man wiped tears from his face with the sleeve of his jacket. Looking up at Nathan with wild eyes, he did not speak.

"Haven't you heard?" Nathan asked. "The war is over. We can all go home now. No need to hide or be afraid."

The boy nodded his head in agreement.

"So what's the problem?"

The dazed look on the lad's face caused Nathan to pursue another avenue.

"I've just cooked some fish," he suggested. "Come have some."

The boy hesitated.

"Come, come," Nathan encouraged.

The boy followed Nathan to the fire and the food. Nathan suddenly wished he'd caught more fish. This boy was really hungry. As Nathan sat eating his own piece of fish, he watched the young man cramming the others into his mouth.

"You got a name?" he asked. "Mine's Nathan."

Appearing to think for a bit, he finally spoke.

"Luke," he said softly. "Luke Prescott."

"Where you from, Luke Prescott?"

"North Carolina. York County, North Carolina."

Luke made no move to leave after they'd eaten, so Nathan just sat easily near the fire and was quiet.

"You one of them Yankees?" Luke asked.

Nathan studied the young face. Clearly he was struggling with some issues.

"The war is over. We're all the same now."

That seemed to satisfy and nothing else was said that evening. Both former soldiers, one from each side of the war, settled in for the night.

Screaming in the middle of the night woke Nathan from a deep sleep. Without thinking, he was on his feet, gun in hand almost before he realized where he was. Luke was having nightmares. Nathan knelt beside him and held him down until he woke in near hysteria.

"It's okay, boy. It's over now," he murmured.

It took Nathan a long time to get back to sleep. When would the war ever truly end?

Nathan didn't mind Luke's company. It was nice to have someone to talk to...when he talked. Mostly they continued in silence. If they talked at all, it was usually about the land they were passing through.

"I don't want to go," Luke burst out without warning.

Nathan looked at Luke. This indeed was a strange young man and Nathan was uneasy at how easily his moods could change.

"Where don't you want to go?"

Luke became very agitated and Nathan was on high alert.

"Home."

Didn't everyone want to go home? Nathan needed to proceed with caution.

"Why is that?"

"I've got to tell her and I don't think I can do that!"

Luke was crying again, something he had done repeatedly the past few days.

"Buddy," Nathan began, "let's sit down over there in the shade and rest a bit."

That seemed like a good idea.

"Now," Nathan continued, "start at the beginning and tell me the whole story. I'm a pretty good listener. Try me."

At first, Nathan thought nothing would be accomplished, but then Luke began to slowly tell the things that haunted his dreams and his waking hours.

"My Dad," he began. "We both was in Atlanta."

Nathan knew what that meant. Atlanta had been brutal.

Luke struggled with the words as he relived the moments.

"I tried to help him. But he got hit. I held him but I couldn't help him," Luke continued, tears streaming down his face, convulsing as he forced the words.

Nathan had flashbacks of holding the dying Red in his arms. He knew the feeling.

"And now I gotta go back and tell Ma. I kept writing like nothing was wrong. I jest couldn't tell her and now I gotta do it or never go back at all."

"Oh, you probably should go back," Nathan said, gently. "I 'spect your Ma'll be mighty glad to see you."

Nathan was holding this young confederate soldier in his arms. His promise to Red to tell Red's little sister was foremost in his mind. He understood all too well and could find no words that would console either one of them.

Finally, Nathan spoke.

"I'll go with you," he said, simply. "Where did you say home is?"

"York County."

"Then York County it is," Nathan said with finality.

19

Grady and Clover

Pea Patch Island. Prison confining confederate soldiers, many captured during the battle of Gettysburg. Its reputation spread quickly among the troops. It rivaled Andersonville in its brutality. Early in the war, Grady Reynolds' zest for battle and the confederacy cause kept him on the move, being somewhat of a free agent and not attached to any particular regiment, always seeking out the thrill of combat. Roaming the southland, he sought out conflicts with the enemy. He became obsessed with the mechanics of war. Now he was obsessed with staying alive in these deplorable surroundings.

Marshy land on the island presented perfect conditions for disease and death. Epidemics of smallpox and measles ran rampant throughout the colony not to mention those issues that came with poor rations and overcrowding. Diarrhea, dysentery and scurvy were every day occurrences as well as infestations of lice. Boats constantly rowed from the island to the mainland with bodies of the dead.

To no one's surprise, Grady became skilled at taking advantage of others' misfortunes. Whether it was being shrewd or having downright disregard for fellow human beings, he twisted grim situations to his own advantage. He pretended friendships and manipulated people to his profit. But in truth, Grady Reynolds trusted no one and had no one's best interests in mind other than his own.

Even though Grady lived by his wits, he suffered from malnutrition and health issues just like the others. But conditions at Pea Patch Island mostly affected Grady's mind. He obsessed about the war, about his beloved plantation, about the Yankee woman who remained there. And his detest for her grew by the day, in fact the very obsession that kept him going. He needed to get back to York County as soon as possible to take control and that would begin when he could leave this island. Complicated plans to escape the prison were always in his thoughts. After two years of confinement, there was little mind or body left of Grady Reynolds.

When news of the end of the war came to Pea Patch Island, he did not experience the joy others had. His was overwhelming emotion at the loss. Failure. Agitation overtook him. The day he walked through the gates and boarded the tiny boat which took him to the mainland found him upset and nervous. One thing was on his mind…getting rid of Samantha Stewart and taking back his beloved plantation.

"Ssh. We haz ta be quiet," Clover urged. "Here, Samuel, you take Aseneth."

Twelve year old Samuel took his four year old sister from his mother's arms and situated her on his back.

Putting Adam behind her with Esau following, then Samuel carrying Aseneth and then ten year old Isaiah was to be last, already having proved he was good at keeping a careful watch, they started through the open field. Bright moonlight lit their path but Clover was aware that same light would be an aid to those who might be following. But Old Marsh said this was the best plan for escape.

It wasn't a huge distance across the field, but they were only part way across it when the sounds of the hounds could be heard in the distance. Coming after Clover and her family or coming after some other family attempting escape? Either way, Clover couldn't chance being caught. The war may have been over on paper, but the hearts of the people still teemed with emotion.

"Run," Clover cautioned as she now kept all her children ahead of her. "To those trees."

The boys ran as fast as their legs could move and Clover kept herself between her children and the ominous sounds coming from behind them. Having made the seclusion of the trees, they crouched together, the sounds of their heavy breathing resonating in the night. If only the hounds had not picked up their scent!

Baying of the hounds and the sound of horses' hooves came closer and fear overtook Clover's body, but the pursuers did not stop and kept going past the cluster of hidden refugees. Even little Aseneth made no noise for the length of time they remained secluded until their mother decided it was safe to move.

They walked for a good portion of the night and Clover began to think her information about a cabin...one that would help them...was incorrect. Finally they came upon a clearing and she could see the outline of a small building. Again they waiting in silence for what seemed like an eternity.

"Samuel," she said, "Ah iz goin' to the door. If this iz not what we're lookin' for and ah does not cum back, you'all take yer brothers and sister and keep workin' yer way north, travelin' only by nighttime 'til you'all find the man called Brother Amos. He be whar the river bends."

"Yessum," Samuel replied as he watched his mother walk stealthily towards the cabin door.

From their hiding place, they could see the door open and the light from a lantern. After a few moments, Clover turned and waved the children to follow. This, then, was their first stop on their way to freedom.

20

Hummingbird Hill,
Mid-May, 1865

She waited throughout the morning hours and into the afternoon. From their hiding place in the cave, Samantha had not observed any sign of the soldiers the entire day. She was pretty sure it was safe to come out of hiding.

"I think it's time," she said simply.

John and Izzy quietly began to gather their belongings.

"No," Samantha cautioned. "It's my job. I'll go down first to assess the situation and see if it's safe. I think it is. I'll send someone for you."

John nodded and Izzy obediently sat down once more cradling a fussing Hope on her lap.

Leading the union soldier's horse outside the cave and taking her pistol with her, she mounted and rode slowly down the hill towards the plantation house lest there be any soldiers left behind. She was correct in her survey of the situation. Union soldiers were gone. She may have been prepared to unexpectedly meet a union soldier, but she was not prepared for the devastation on every side as she walked the horse through the plantation yard. An eerie calm seemed to penetrate the atmosphere, like the calm one experiences after a storm.

Waves of surprise, sadness, devastation and anger washed over her as she saw broken windows, doors completely gone or hanging at an angle. Household items strewn all over the yard. The smokehouse had been ransacked, doors ripped off their hinges and left on the ground as a reminder of the strength of an army. She was pretty sure there would be no hams, bacon, or fowl left in there.

Fences were torn down and tender cotton plants trampled beyond belief. Turning the horse towards the cabins, she saw faces peering at her from the windows.

Callie was the first to appear.

"Miz Samantha," she wailed. "We wuz so scared. They wuz too many of 'em. We couldn't do anythin' but watch. They wuz mean, they wuz."

"I know," Samantha said calmly. "Was anyone hurt? Are all accounted for?"

"Mah Elijah got hiz leg hurt when he tried to save the horses," Callie continued. "Clover...she and her kidz...they be gone. Haven't seed John. No Izzy."

"John, Izzy and Hope are safe," Samantha explained.

She was not surprised about Clover's absence. Hadn't she just been looking for an excuse to leave? In her inner self, Samantha was not angry about it. Actually, she was somewhat relieved.

"Callie, send Moses up the hill. There is a cave up there and John and Izzy and Hope are safe inside it. Tell them it's alright to come on down. And tell them to bring the prisoner."

Callie's eyes grew big and round at that news, but she followed instructions. Soon all the darkies were assembled in the side yard and Samantha quickly organized them into groups. Field hands would return to the cotton fields to try to salvage what they could of the cotton crop. Household slaves would help Samantha in the house and yards. Before long, children were finding and catching the remainder of the chickens that were scattered and putting them back in the pen Aaron was repairing. After Elijah's leg had been given medical attention, he and Aaron took the soldier's horse and rode off to see if they could find any of the stable horses that might not have strayed too far.

Samantha was not prepared for the utter destruction she saw in the house. Hoof prints were evident on the fine hardwood floors where union troops had ridden their horses through the house. It was as if an ill wind had swept through the rooms.

Callie wailed and cried as she gathered up cooking utensils and sorted broken kitchen items, finding what was salvageable. Eggs and molasses and broken dishes strewn over the floor were the first things to be cleaned. After walking in a daze through the house,

Samantha and Izzy and Miriam started sweeping up broken glass and pieces of furniture from the library. It seemed like the best place to start. Bottles from the liquor cabinet were drained and strewn on the library floor. Books had been pulled from their shelves and trampled underfoot. Pictures were torn from the walls. The portrait of Samantha lay broken in the grand entrance hall. It was heartbreaking work, each discovery of destruction bringing more tears. Senseless damage. Senseless ruin.

Day three dawned. The kitchen was functioning…limited, but functioning…and several horses had been located and brought back to the stables. Elijah was patiently working to repair the damage on the barn and the wagons, making do with what little he had to work with. A decent flock of hens had been caught and confined and would soon be laying eggs again. Two milk cows had been found and brought back to their corral. And the yearling calf showed up on its own. The hogs were a different story. They preferred the wild.

As many plants had been salvaged from the garden and replanted as was possible. The smoke house door had been repaired, but Samantha was correct in her assessment. Meats that had been hung there were gone. Apparently no one had thought to ransack the cellar so there was still a supply of yams and root vegetables as well as other items stored there. Samantha was thankful the water in the well had not been tampered with and the house had not been burned. It could have been worse.

Today laundry tubs were found and fires built under the huge kettles and several of the house slaves had laundry under way. Delicious aromas coming once again from the kitchen were a boost to weary spirits.

Samantha caught a glimpse of herself as she passed one of the broken mirrors still clinging to the wall. Smudges of dirt covered her face and her hair was askew, but the hollowness of her eyes reflecting the desolation she felt inside was absolutely terrifying. She was shocked by her own appearance. No longer was she the mistress of the plantation; she was a woman trying to survive.

When she couldn't stand the overwhelming confusion and destruction inside the house, she walked around the yards and gardens. Exhausted and discouraged, she constantly fought the possibility of tears. As she stood leaning against the fence near the barn, thinking she should have Elijah saddle a horse so she could ride away from the mess for a while, she noticed a figure coming up the lane. Seldom were there guests these days, especially one traveling on foot. She squinted in the sunlight to see whoever might be walking in this bright spring sunshine.

It was not easy leaving Pa Rice and Rob. They had been good to Chase, nurturing him back to health, literally bringing him back from death's door. But Chase was eager to be on the move again. Spring had arrived; and with it, he could feel the renewal of life all around him as he walked the meadows and hillsides.

"Hello, stranger," Chase's thoughts were interrupted by the salutation.

A man in a wagon pulled his team of horses to a halt.

"Hello," Chase returned the greeting.

"Have you heard the news?" the stranger asked.

"What news is that?" Chase inquired. "I've been sort of out of touch with things as of late."

"Lee surrendered at Appomattox," he offered. "The war is over."

Relief flowed through Chase's body. Finally the fighting had subsided.

"That's good news...that the war is over," Chase said cautiously, not knowing whether the end of the war coincided with the man's political views.

It seemed to make no difference.

"Perhaps you could tell me," Chase began. "I am on my way to York County. Not familiar with the territory. Am I close?"

"Sure are," the stranger offered.

Apparently political views were of no consequence.

"The Catawba River is about ten miles ahead of ya. York County's just on the other side."

Chase's heart leaped at the prospect of being so near his year long journey.

"But," the stranger added, "I need ta tell ya. The trestle bridge has been blown away. You'll have ta ford the river. And it's a might high this time of year."

"Thanks," Chase muttered. "Any chance you'd be familiar with the Hummingbird Hill plantation?"

"Naw, can't say as I am. Maybe somebody down at the river could help ya out."

"Okay. Thanks."

With a wave of his hand and a clucking noise to the team of horses, the man went on his way and Chase started off at a brisk walk. Ten more miles to the river. Samantha couldn't be much farther.

The stranger was correct. Chase reached the Catawba the following day and was given directions for fording the river and for finding Hummingbird Hill.

When he saw the wooden sign for Hummingbird Hill near the edge of the lane, even though one side of it had fallen down from the iron rings that held the sign in place, Chase could not help but feel a surge in his body. He wasn't sure if it was relief or joy or just what the emotion was. Was it possible after all this time his beloved sister was nearby?

As he stood at the sign near the entrance to the lane lined with trees on each side, he saw the magnificent white flowers with their waxy dark green leaves sparkling in the sun. Magnolia trees! Magnolia trees in bloom! What had Samantha's letter said? *It's particularly beautiful when magnolias are in bloom!*

Chase hastened his step.

Samantha was curious about the man walking up the lane. At first, she thought there was something familiar about the way he walked, but she really didn't think she knew anyone who walked with a limp. But she couldn't be sure and she needed to be cautious. Good land, these days there were enough changes going on! Where once she had welcomed guests, now her openness was more reserved. She thought about getting her pistol, but this man didn't seem to exude any kind of threat. As he approached, she could see he was slender in build and had several day's growth of beard on his face. Still there was something about the way he carried himself...and the color of his hair, although long, was strangely familiar. She turned, taking time to brush the hair back from her dirty face, and slowly walked towards him. Something inside her told her it was the thing to do as she hurried to meet him.

He had waited as long as he could.

"Samantha?" he called out.

Her heart swelled as she ran towards him, forgetting the smudges on her cheeks, forgetting the fact that her clothes were torn and dirty and she hadn't bathed for days.

His arms were opened wide and she flowed into them.

"Chase! Chase! Is it really you?"

"It's me, little sister," he said. "A little worse for wear, but it's me."

She alternated hugging him and kissing him and then she just needed to look into his eyes.

"Oh, how I've missed you," she purred. "How many times I've wanted to talk with you!"

"I know the feeling," he said, once again pulling her to him.

"How did you get here? Why are you walking? Are you alone? Mama...and Papa...are they alright? Tell me everything."

"Whoa," Chase said. "It's a long story."

"Of course," she realized. "You must be tired. Sit and rest a bit. But I want to hear every detail."

They turned, arm in arm, to walk towards the house.

"What has happened here?" he said, gazing around at the debris and damage.

"Soldiers," she said, sadly. "Union soldiers came through and demolished everything."

"Why now?" Chase said. "I understand the war is over."

"Really? We hadn't heard. Really? Finally over?"

It was as if a burden had been lifted. But it was followed by the descending of a huge weight. Grady. What about Grady?

Chase continued talking, pretending he hadn't felt the fear that had suddenly gripped her.

"That's what I understand. Everyone I've come in contact with the past couple of days has said the same thing. Lee surrendered to Grant at Appomattox. Soldiers are on their way home."

It was something Samantha had not thought about recently. Soldiers coming home. Grady coming home.

Trying not to notice the look of panic on Samantha's face, Chase continued.

"Well, this isn't quite the grand picture of Hummingbird Hill you painted in your letters, but show me around the place."

Chase grinned and Samantha relaxed for the first time in a long time.

They walked together through the rubble. He winced when he saw the portrait of Samantha in shambles. In his mind, he pictured the plantation house as it might have been as she walked and told him how things used to be. However, they hadn't been apart so long that he didn't pick up on the fact that every time she mentioned Grady's name, something didn't seem quite right.

Even though the dining room was in shambles, Samantha insisted they eat properly. By propping up the broken leg of the dining room table, she and Chase dined on the best food Callie could scrape together. By candlelight, Samantha could still see the weariness in Chase's face. Well, this war had aged everyone. She listened with great interest as he shared stories of his journey and told her of his experiences with the armies, being captured, about Mac, about Oma and Pa Rice and his son, Rob.

"Nathan saved my life," he said simply.

Samantha raised her eyebrows.

"I was running away after I had been accused of being a spy and I heard the soldiers coming but didn't know where to hide. Then Nathan's words came to me just like when we were kids and I was able to find refuge in a tree. It was something we had done together as boys."

"Nathan has been with me as well," she said wistfully. "It is amazing the strength we pull from our memories."

She seemed lost in thought as they continued their meal in silence.

"Mother is not well," he said as they finished their meal.

He had Samantha's attention.

"I was sent down here to bring you back home."

She was quiet and he couldn't read the emotion in her face.

"How bad is it?"

"Bad enough. The doctor says he can't predict. Personally, I think some of her problems are because she has worried about you since the outbreak of the war. And the doctor agrees with that as well."

She seemed to dismiss his words, almost as if she hadn't heard them or chose to ignore them.

"How is Nathan?" she asked, a noticeable change in subject.

Noticing her reticence to talk about their mother, he continued.

"We had one letter from him before I left Washington. He signed up right away, you know…for the war."

That news appeared to surprise her.

"No, I didn't know."

"It was never the same after you left, Samantha. He and I still did things together but it was like something had left him."

A deep sadness crossed her face.

"And I think that something was you, Samantha."

"Surely I was never that important to him," she replied, feeling tears beginning to well up in her eyes.

"I wouldn't be too sure about that. I think he always thought the two of you would marry."

"That's what I thought, too," she said wistfully. "Now look at me. We're not children anymore with wild dreams for our future."

Samantha looked around at the debris in the plantation dining room and Chase thought for a bit she might cry.

"Don't lose sight of your dreams, Samantha," he encouraged.

A slight smile crossed her face and she spoke with a renewed spirit.

"I believe Callie has made sweet potato pie for dessert," she said.

Sleeping underneath the stars had taken on an entirely different meaning for Nathan. There was no smell of gunpowder, no fear of being awakened to the threat of being shot. The sky was such a lovely shade of dark blue sprinkled with a dusting of stars and there was a slight indication that the moon might make an appearance to dispel the clouds. Such a beautiful night! Another night of dreaming about Samantha and being back in Washington, when life was about laughter and fun.

Luke Prescott was already sleeping nearby. His nightmares had decreased over the past few days. Nathan was glad to have his companionship and felt good about escorting the boy back to York County, North Carolina. He felt his company had a healing effect on the lad.

Nathan turned on his side and slept a peaceful sleep.

Luke and Nathan had not gone far the next morning when Nathan took hold of Luke's arm.

"Wait," he said, cautiously. "Look there."

Luke followed Nathan's direction to see a horse standing in the tall grass, fully saddled and bridled. Nathan approached the horse with Luke following close behind him.

"There now," he said softly as he neared the horse and the horse moved slightly away from him.

Nathan reached for the bridle; and taking hold of it, he ran his hands over the horse's body to see if there was an injury of some kind. There was none. He began to look around for the rider.

"What do ya think?" Luke whispered.

"Don't know," Nathan replied. "Rider must be somewhere close by. Horse is ground reined."

No one was in sight; so with reins in hand, Nathan began walking in circles to see if he could find the owner.

"Here," Luke called out. "Over here!"

Nathan responded as Luke stood over a body crumpled on the ground. Nathan rolled the man over.

"He dead?" Luke asked.

Nathan nodded.

"Sure is. Bullet right through the head."

He looked around further, half expecting someone to jump out after them; but there was no movement anywhere and no one was in sight.

They did the best they could at making a burial for the stranger.

"Misfortune for one sometimes leads to fortune for another," Nathan said. "Looks like we got ourselves a horse."

It was easier going whether they rode double or whether one walked and one rode. Now it would take less time to get Luke to York County and less time before Nathan would make his way back to Washington, D. C.

Chase lay awake in one of the upstairs bedrooms in the plantation house. It was comfortable in spite of the destruction. Surely better sleeping in a bed than on the hard ground. And once again his stomach was satisfied with food. Southern life was different alright. He had never experienced the darkies moving about. Now that the war was over, Samantha would have some tough decisions to make. He was proud of his little sister for having carried such a heavy burden with Grady gone. And what about Grady? She hadn't talked much about him. Rather she seemed to cloud up when Grady's name was mentioned.

Would Samantha even want to come back to Washington with him? He hadn't considered that. Well, he wouldn't push her. He sensed she'd had enough conflict for a while. Instead, he decided he would stay for a while and do what he could to help restore the plantation. At least he'd stay for a few days. Good to be with Samantha again plus this bed felt so good.

Chase turned to blow out the candle next to his bed. The last thing he heard before he slept was the sound of the slaves and their mournful songs coming from the cabins.

———————— ❧❧❧ ————————

Samantha adjusted the bedding on her bed for the third time. She had turned from side to side for hours now and still sleep just wouldn't come. It was wonderful having Chase here. But Chase's presence had stirred up feelings again of Nathan. The news of mother's poor health bothered her. And now that the war was declared over, she would have to deal with the slavery issue. But, most of all, the end of the war could possibly mean that Grady would be coming back. And then what? What would she do when Grady came back into her life again?

21

Summer 1865

"What's going on here?" Chase inquired of the soldier shackled to the garden fence.

"We captured him."

Chase laughed.

"I always knew how strong you were, but apprehending union soldiers? That's quite a feat for any woman...even if you are my little sister."

"Well, something good ought to have come from hanging out with you and Nathan," she retorted.

"Seriously, how did you manage that?"

"He made the mistake of coming back alone to look for us while we were in the cave hiding from the troops. Got just a might too close. John and I managed to attack him from both sides. I was terrified to think the others would return to look for him and find our hiding place."

"That's my little sister...always resourceful!"

They laughed together, amazed at the realization of how long it had been for each of them.

"What are you going to do with him?"

"Oh, my goodness, I suppose if the war is over, he should be set free."

"I don't think there's anyone or any place around here where we can take him. What do you think?"

"I guess we just turn him loose. When I've talked to him, I think he's just like most men in the war. He just wants to go home to his family."

Chase nodded as they walked together towards the prisoner and set about untying the soldier.

"You're free to go," Samantha told him. "The war is over and you can be on your way home. Go to the kitchen and Callie will give you some food for your journey."

A grateful young man headed towards the plantation house.

"Chase, I am so glad you're here. Things are easier when we are together."

"Looks to me like you've managed to have everything under control without me," he complimented. "But there's the issue of the slaves. Have you thought about that?"

"The slaves have been one of my biggest concerns since I've been here. Really only one has given me problems and she has run away with her children. And I say good riddance, although Grady would probably disagree."

There it was again, the distant tone in her voice when she talked of Grady.

"Clover and her children are worth a lot of money. At least they were before the war. And some...Izzy and Callie and her family...are like family to me. They've all helped in putting things back together after the invasion, not because they had to, but because they wanted to."

Right now there was more clean up to be done and there was no way that would happen without major effort on the part of everyone. By the end of the day, more progress would be made and now Chase was here and that made all the difference.

White blossoms nestled between beautiful waxy deep green leaves dotted the landscape. Magnolias had started their magnificent display of color. The southland was waking up to a day of repair and recovery. Nathan found himself fully engrossed in the beauty before him.

"Wait," Luke said as he stopped to scan the countryside.

"What is it?" Nathan inquired, bringing the horse to a halt.

"I think we're getting close to the plantation. Things are starting to look familiar to me."

That was good news. Nathan was anxious to put some serious miles between the battlefields and home.

"Good," he said. "Let's press on."

Within two days, Nathan could feel the tenseness growing in Luke as the two continued their journey.

"It will be alright," Nathan encouraged. "Your mother will be hurt and sad, but she will go on just like you have to go on. Life will never be the same, but the sun will continue to come up every morning just like the good Lord promised."

Still unsure, Luke shook his head, once again in fear of being overcome with emotion.

About noon they crossed a small creek and made their way over a gentle rise in the land and then there before them was the Prescott plantation.

"It looks the same," Luke exclaimed as they approached, seemingly relieved that his home was intact.

"And there's my mother standing in the yard!" he exclaimed as he broke into a run.

Nathan kept a steady pace while Luke ran ahead of him. Nancy Prescott, seeing her son coming from afar, ran towards him and Nathan watched as the two embraced. He fought his own emotions at that point, visions of a reunion with his own family foremost in his mind. Nathan sat quietly atop the horse realizing the Prescotts…mother and son…were hardly aware of his approach.

"Oh, Mother," Luke said, finally realizing Nathan was there. "This is my good friend, Nathan. He was kind enough to share my journey…and my sorrow."

Luke knew it was time. He turned to his mother with tears in his eyes, once again entering her embrace.

"It's father," he wept. "Oh, it's father!"

"I know, I know," Nancy Prescott consoled.

Luke looked into his mother's eyes.

"How could you know?"

"I haven't heard from him for a very long time. I suspicioned, but I think I knew all along in my heart he was gone."

Once again, mother and son cried together. Nathan knew everything would be alright now for Luke. The healing would come.

"Where are my manners?" Nancy Prescott said, wiping her eyes on the white embroidered handkerchief, a symbol of civilization in this uncivilized destruction. "Come on in, Nathan. You boys must be hungry and Delilah has just made a chicken pot pie."

"Thank you kindly, ma'am," Nathan replied, hardly able to control the feelings in his stomach at the thought of some home cooking.

Nathan relished the food placed before him from the chicken pot pie and greens to the sweet potato pie with cream and had to remind himself that no matter how hungry one was, he should eat like he was not. Fortunately for him, Luke and his mother were so deeply engrossed in conversation they hardly noticed when he took a third portion.

"And where do you hail from, Nathan?" Nancy Prescott asked.

Caught with a mouthful of pie, Nathan had to wait to respond.

"Washington, D. C., ma'am," he answered.

"Ah do want to thank you for escorting mah son back to York County," she said.

"It appears that York County escaped much of the fighting."

"Yes. The train trestle over the Catawba is about the only confrontation we had. Although the union troops swept through here several weeks ago. Our plantation is so small, it was overlooked, but I fear Hummingbird Hill just to the west of us received much damage."

Had he heard correctly? Hummingbird Hill? Could it be? He needed to know more.

"And, exactly where would Hummingbird Hill be located, ma'am?" he asked, feeling the excitement course through his body.

"Whah just a few miles northwest of here."

"What family lives there?"

"It's Grady Reynolds' plantation. He has not been heard from for ovah a year now. And poor Samantha, his wife, has been running the plantation bah herself. Ah know she is a strong and capable young woman, but it still must be a terrible strain on her. Ah've not been there lately mahself but ah've heard about the damage the union troops have caused and ah imagine she is devastated."

Nathan's Samantha? Was it even possible the spirited young partner of his youth was this close to him?

"I need to go there," he blurted out.

Luke looked at him suspiciously, feeling the need for an explanation.

"I do believe I know the lady of the plantation," Nathan faltered with the words. "How long will it take me to get there?"

"Ah would think about an hour...bah horseback," Nancy Prescott volunteered.

His chair scraped against the floor as he pushed back from the table. Tired as he may have been, he could surely push another hour to reach Samantha.

"Surely you can wait 'til mornin'," Luke suggested.

"Yes, do. A good night's sleep would be beneficial," Nancy Prescott persuaded.

"I do thank you kindly, ma'am...Luke...but I need to move on."

Getting general directions to Hummingbird Hill, Nathan mounted the horse once more and pressed on to his destination. Thoughts of Samantha filled his head, not only thoughts of her as a young and flirtatious girl in Washington but also thoughts of a Samantha transplanted and attempting to survive in a difficult situation.

Trees flew by as Nathan urged the horse over new terrain. He was saddle weary, his hair was long and stringy, his clothes were filthy but he gave little thought to those things. Every step of the horse's hooves brought him closer to Samantha. Cotton fields stretched to his left and he could hear the rush of water to his right. And then before him was the sign...Hummingbird Hill, now repaired and hanging properly. He had finally arrived!

It was as if every magnolia blossom heralded his arrival. Dusk was beginning to descend and yet the white flowers of the magnolia trees on either side of him lining the lane to the house stood out in bright contrast. He walked the horse now, staring in wonderment as the magnificent trees stood shoulder to shoulder welcoming him. Up ahead, he could see several small glimmers of light coming from the house. As he reached the end of the lane leading to the plantation house, he pulled his horse to a stop.

"Hello," he shouted. "Is anyone there?"

His heart was pounding in his chest. It seemed like an eternity before he saw the double doors of the house open and a man step from it.

"What is it you want?" the man asked.

A man? That voice certainly did not remind him of Grady Reynolds, but it sounded familiar.

"I am looking for friends," Nathan replied.

"Who is it you seek?" Chase asked, squinting in the poor lighting at the figure on horseback.

"I am looking for Samantha Stewart," he said.

The use of Samantha's maiden name surprised Chase. Just then Samantha appeared at Chase's side.

"Who is it, Chase?" she whispered.

"Not sure," he replied.

Samantha felt for the pistol at her side. Raising it, she leveled it at the intruder.

"Perhaps you need to keep right on moving."

Nathan raised his hands above his head.

"Hey," he said, "I didn't teach you how to shoot one of those just to have you shoot me."

Had she heard correctly? Could it possibly be?

"Samantha."

"Nathan."

The sound of his voice was like a healing balm to her soul. Leaving Chase's side, she rushed towards the figure as he dismounted. She was in his arms and he lifted her from the ground and swung her around. Holding Samantha was the best feeling in all the world.

She was crying and hugging him all at the same time.

"Where…how…is it really you?"

He smiled.

"It's me," he whispered. "It's been a long journey."

She hugged him again and again.

"Hey, it's my turn," Chase interrupted.

Samantha released him long enough for Chase and Nathan to embrace and then she immediately was in his arms again.

"What are you doing here?" Nathan asked of Chase.

"It's a long story," Chase admitted. "And you showing up here...how could that happen?"

Samantha interrupted.

"We have a lot to talk about," she said. "Come in. Are you hungry? We hadn't heard from you for such a long time. We didn't know..." her voice trailed off.

"There's a lot to catch up on," Nathan said. "Tonight, it's just enough to be together."

They walked arm in arm towards the house...the three of them...together once again. The candles burned down low, conversation flowed, emotions ran at peak levels and the smell of magnolias wafted through the house.

22

After the War

Wind whipped against his face as he forced the horse faster and faster covering the miles to York County and Hummingbird Hill. Well, the farmer he stole the horse from wouldn't miss him…at least for a time. When that horse gave out, he would find another to use. Haste was of the utmost importance now. Grady's mind built scenarios of what he would find upon his return to York County. He was filled with anger and revenge and rage. The confederacy had fallen. His beloved south would never be the same. Grady Reynolds would never be the same.

He hadn't slept for days, his bleary eyes proof of that. Sleep could wait. He found food where he could at any farm or byway but it didn't seem to make much progress against his now gaunt frame. Sheer determination had kept his body from succumbing to the perils of prison encampment, but it hadn't kept his mind healthy.

A crazed Grady Reynolds raced cross country on his way to Hummingbird Hill.

"Have you noticed anything peculiar about Samantha?" Chase asked.

"Well, I've noticed that she's matured into a woman, if that's what you mean," Nathan answered.

"No, I mean whenever Grady's name is brought up in conversation."

Nathan thought a bit. Had he noticed a change in her demeanor at the mention of her husband's name or did he just want to find some little bit of something?

"I thought it was my imagination," he finally said.

Chase stopped working on the window he was attempting to repair.

"It's more than imagination," he concluded. "And it's been that way since I got here. I think something is definitely wrong."

Nathan wiped the perspiration from his face, images of a restrained Grady ranting in the Yankee camp fresh in his mind.

"Have you asked her about it?"

"No."

Chase hoisted the window and Nathan picked up the hammer as they worked together to put the window in its place.

It was at the breakfast table the following morning that she made her announcement.

"I will start packing today," she said. "We should be ready to leave for home in a few of days."

Chase was astounded at the abruptness of her decision.

"What will you do about the plantation?" he asked.

"It was never mine to begin with," she retorted.

And was that bitterness in her voice?

"You don't intend to wait for Grady's return?"

Color rose in Samantha's face. There was a definite coldness in her voice when she spoke.

"I have not heard from him for a long time now. Who knows where he might be...if indeed he is still alive."

Nathan's mind leaped back to the prisoner he encountered months ago and the braggart Grady Reynolds. Should he tell her? Would it help if she knew? After all, Nathan really didn't know what had happened to Grady Reynolds after he was taken prisoner. But he did know he had been captured.

That evening, when they were alone, Nathan shared what he knew of Grady with Chase.

Chase listened intently to the story and the degrading things Grady had said about his sister.

"I don't know how she would react to the news," he concluded. "Maybe best to wait. I feel like we will know when the time is right."

Anyone within a few feet of him would begin to wonder about the wild man who raced over the countryside. He muttered words aloud as he relived battles from the past three years, shouted orders to men who were no longer there to obey them. He urged his horse faster as if he were going into battle, his eyes reflecting the torment of his mind. Grady had hardly stopped long enough to eat and only took time to locate another horse when the one he had driven to death collapsed underneath him.

Despite the fact he appeared to be insane, his mind had not given up on his goal, his destination. His treasured Hummingbird Hill was always first and foremost in his thoughts. No battle he had encountered during the war matched the one that raged within him now.

"It's a place I've often visited since I've been in York County," she explained as they pulled their horses to a stop atop the ridge that overlooked the Catawba River.

Taking a break from the tedium of putting the plantation back together, Nathan and Samantha had gone for a horseback ride. She really did want him to see the beauty of the country.

"I like this spot because I can see the plantation in one direction and the river in the other. The river gives me a feeling of freedom. Strange, isn't it? In an atmosphere of slavery that *I* should be the one seeking freedom as well."

He looked at her, but her eyes did not meet his.

"There are many types of slavery," he said softly. "All kinds of things that keep us prisoner."

"But sometimes the answer lies within ourselves."

She gazed into the distance. Had she heard his words? Should he bring up the subject of Grady at this time? Would she consider her relationship with Grady none of his business?

"Samantha," he began but did not finish.

"You've been wondering why I do not mention Grady," she interrupted as if she had read the question he was about to ask.

"Well, I..." he stuttered and then gained boldness. "Yes, as a matter of fact, that has confused me a bit."

He saw the set of her jaw and the bitterness in her eyes.

"Hatred is a really bad feeling," she said solemnly.

There was an uncomfortable pause.

"I have never experienced hatred before."

"I do not see you as being a hateful person, if you are talking about yourself."

"I hate what I know of slavery and I hate that I have not been the wife he expected."

Conflicting emotions ran rampant through Nate's body.

"Samantha," he began, "you do not have to..."

She turned towards him with tears in her eyes.

"Yes, I have to," she explained. "And there's no one I'd rather share this awful secret with than you."

Tears trickled down her cheeks. Nathan reached over to put his hand on hers.

"No one knows what kind of a man he really is," she continued.

Nathan caught his breath. He had a good idea after witnessing Grady's outburst in the union camp.

"Not only me . . . but humiliating me with the black women slaves. And then my precious little Izzy. That's rape, Nathan, pure and simple."

Nathan felt sick to his stomach.

"He doesn't deserve you," he consoled.

"Maybe I don't deserve any better," she anguished through her tears, finally giving way to the stress of the past five years.

"Now that's just not true," Nathan was vehement. "You are a wonderful, kind, intelligent woman. He's a fool to think anything else."

"And I don't even know if he's alive or dead or what."

"Did he ever hurt you, Samantha? I mean, physically."

"Mostly verbal. He did push and slap me, but only once."

Only once? Once was one time too many.

Nathan thought for a moment as he watched the river rolling below them. The war had lasted most of five years and lives had been changed forever; and yet, the Catawba continued on its voyage just as it had for all the years before and would continue in the years to come.

"I saw him," he said softly.

She turned towards him in disbelief and stared at him through red eyes.

"You...you saw him?"

He struggled with the words to tell her. But it was time.

"He and two other prisoners spent one night in our camp, probably a year ago, maybe more."

The look in Samantha's eyes demanded more information.

"He was bragging and arrogant. I wasn't sure it was him until I took him by surprise calling out his name. When he reacted to it, I knew it was him."

He paused.

"...and I reacted, too. All I wanted to do was to pound him into the ground."

He was agitated.

"No, I will not give you all the details," he said. "Grady Reynolds is a selfish, mean spirited man; and if he never comes back into your life, you should consider yourself fortunate."

"Do you know what happened to him?"

What was this? Did she still care about him? Is that why she wanted to know more? Or was it merely curiosity? Nathan found himself wishing he hadn't said anything. But he answered her question calmly.

"No, I don't. He was taken with the other two prisoners that were captured with him and a detail picked them up the next morning. Most likely he went to one of the prison camps."

"They...the camps...are bad, aren't they?"

"I don't know. Have only heard tales...but, yes, from all reports, they are horrific."

He quickly added, "But if anyone could survive those conditions, it would be Grady Reynolds."

Was that what she wanted to hear? After everything she'd gone through, did she want Grady back in her life?

By his calculations, Grady Reynolds could not be more than a day's ride from Hummingbird Hill. If there was one thing his stay at Pea Island had taught him, it was perseverance. The stench of the camp continued to fill his nostrils. The swamp like conditions only added to the sickness. Suffering from smallpox, measles, diarrhea, dysentery, scurvy and lice was vivid in his mind. Even now his stomach lurched at the thought of sickness and death all around. He'd lost count after the first week of those who were transported to the mainland for burial. Now he was giddy with freedom from it all. But would he ever be free? The imprisonment had torn something from Grady's soul and replaced it with irrational thoughts.

Driving rain beat down on him and the horse he'd ridden nonstop for the past twenty four hours. The rain had lasted that long, too; and the road which was merely a path had turned to a river of mud. Without warning, the horse lost its footing and fell, throwing Grady to the ground. Screams of pain from the animal pierced the night air. A single shot rang out to relieve the suffering.

And now Grady Reynolds was walking alone across soggy ground in unrelenting torrents of rain.

——————— ⌜◯∞◯⌝ ———————

Chase chose to ignore Samantha's tear stained face when she and Nathan returned from their ride. But something had changed, something positive. She suddenly wanted to know the details of their mother's illness. Samantha was industrious once again, making plans to head back north to Washington, D. C. and her family.

Since the news of the end of the war, Samantha had been concerned about the slaves and what would happen to them…and what Grady's reaction would be to any decision Samantha might make if and when he returned from the war.

It was a confusing time, not only for Samantha, but for the slaves who lived on the plantation. Some of the darkies had left to try to reunite with family somewhere else in the south. Only Callie and Elijah and their children and John, Izzy and Hope remained.

Men from larger cities from both the north and the south, hoping to take advantage of the situation, had come by to make offers on plantation property and Samantha was considering a proposal for the sale of the plantation. But, remembering the teachings of her father and the caution he had instilled in her, Samantha sought the advice of Mr. Hall, attorney at law.

"Thank you for seeing me, Mr. Hall," she said, extending her hand to the funny little man in the brown suit.

Mr. Hall had been doing legal work for the Reynolds' family for quite some time and was more than impressed by the young Mrs. Reynolds' beauty and intelligence.

"What can I do for you today, Mrs. Reynolds?" he said as he gestured towards a chair for her comfort.

"Thank you. As you probably well know, plantation owners are being readily approached by a number of buyers from the city."

Mr. Hall nodded.

"I would like to take advantage of their offers."

Mr. Hall raised his eyebrows in surprise.

"You want to sell the plantation? Samantha, I don't know as you can legally do that."

"Yes. Grady has been gone to the war for several years now and I have not heard from him and fear the worst has happened to him. My plans are to return to my family in Washington. But I want a fair price for the property. I do not want to just give it away. I want you to check into the matter to see if I, as a widow, would have any rights."

Mr. Hall cleared his throat and adjusted his spectacles on his face and shuffled some papers on his desk.

"This is a huge step," he said. "Have you considered…uh, Mr. Reynolds could still return…it's awfully soon to make a decision…"

Samantha waved her hand to dismiss his attempt to dissuade her.

"Yes, Mr. Hall, I've thought this through and I'm quite sure about what I want to do."

She saw resignation in his face.

"Well, if you are sure," he said. "I will look into the matter and if you are legally responsible, I can give you the name of a reputable man who would be fair with you. But the chances are…"

"Yes," she agreed. "That's what I want."

She paused.

"However," she continued. "There is one further piece of business I wish for you to handle. There is a part of Hummingbird Hill I wish to deed to one of my slaves."

Now Samantha really had Mr. Hall's attention.

"Oh, that sort of thing is not done," he hesitated. "Highly irregular."

Mr. Hall, attorney at law, became quite agitated.

"No, that sort of thing is just not done."

But as he continued to object, he knew his efforts were futile.

"Oh, of that I am sure, Mr. Hall. Nevertheless, I would like to follow through with that document as well. There is one piece of land…good farming land with a few fruit trees and plenty of water and I want it deeded to John and Izzy. I realize it is an unusual request but it is what I want to do. As you might recall, that piece of property *is* in my name."

"I'll send someone out right away," he resigned.

All Mr. Hall could do was to offer advice. In the end, he was obligated to obey his clients' wishes. He would start immediately to accommodate Mrs. Reynolds' plans.

Cotton needed tending in the fields, but mostly work on the plantation these days was to care for the animals and the garden so there would be food to eat. And food to eat there was. Several hogs had been captured due to Elijah's slyness and Aaron's quickness and butchering had taken place. Both Chase and Nathan added to their weight daily and appeared to gain strength each day.

Grady lost track of the days. He had been walking for several before he found any kind of civilization. And now he was underway again with a fresh horse. If only the farmer hadn't resisted allowing Grady to take the horse! Then he would still be alive, but shooting one more person wouldn't make any difference now. Grady Reynolds needed to get to his beloved Hummingbird Hill and killing had become second nature to him.

"Why do women have so much stuff?" Nathan complained as he and Chase helped Aaron and Moses load the last of the travel trunks into the back of the wagon.

Elijah brought the carriage up behind the wagon with Nate's horse tied behind and John heaved the last of the smaller bags behind the driver's seat.

"Where is she?" Chase questioned impatiently.

"You know women," Nathan laughed. "Always taking their time."

At that particular moment, Samantha came through the repaired front doors onto the porch, stepping from the darkness of the plantation house into the bright morning sunlight.

"She still takes my breath away," Nathan murmured as he watched her descend the porch steps.

Chase put an understanding and sympathetic hand on Nathan's shoulder.

Indeed, Samantha was an elegant sight to behold, dressed in her pink and green striped dress with matching bag and white gloves, and parasol to keep the bright sun from her delicate skin. Dark hair peeked out from under the picture hat she wore and her eyes danced once more at the thought of returning to Washington D. C. and family.

It was a beautiful summer morning, still cool before the intense heat of the day set in. The dark green leaves of the magnolias glistened in the morning light as the petals of the flowers unfolded at the sun's request. A respectable amount of replanted cotton plants was once again growing in the fields. Although there were many repairs yet to be made, debris from the union invasion had been mostly cleaned up. The welcome sounds of a cow lowing in the pasture and the clucking of hens as they scratched for food permeated the air.

Turning her back on Hummingbird Hill was more difficult than she had imagined. Standing near the front porch were Elijah and Callie and Miriam with John, Izzy and Hope. Moses and Aaron stood holding the bridles of the horses. They were all that was left of the darkies and now they were set free. The tail of Callie's apron silently wiped her eyes and Izzy's tears ran freely down her cheeks. Even John and Moses and Aaron hung their heads.

One of the horses snorted and shifted his weight, eager to be on his way.

Well, this is it, Samantha thought as she drank in the picture before her.

 Chase and Nathan stood silently watching her, each man with his own set of thoughts.

Putting her hand bag over her arm, Samantha started towards Izzy for one last goodbye when the peaceful scene was interrupted by the sound of horses hooves coming at a dead run down the lane of magnolias. Its rider was waving his arm in the air and shouting. All eyes turned towards the figure.

Grady brought the lathered horse to a halt. Waving his saber above his head, he demanded.

"What is going on hehr, pray tell," he shouted. "Has the enemy passed by this way? There are troops crossing the river as we speak. Take cover or be killed!"

The group of witnesses stood dumbstruck.

"Oh, ah see," he continued. "*You* are the enemy! And this is mah plantation. Ya' all are intruders. Ah see that ya'all are union and therefore the enemy."

Nathan was the first to speak.

"Sir, the war is over. There is to be no more killing. There is no more union or confederate."

Grady's eyes blazed with hatred as he wielded the sabre. Its swishing sound as it cut through the air sent chills through the spectators.

"How dare you! Ya'll have come to take possession of mah beloved plantation and ah will not allow it. Prepare to die!"

With that he urged his horse towards the unarmed Nathan, but Nathan was quick to step aside and Grady plunged his sabre into the side of the wagon. The jar knocked him from his horse. He quickly got to his feet as Nathan dislodged the sword to protect himself from this madman.

Samantha distracted him by walking towards them.

"What is it you want?" she asked with all the control she could muster.

Grady took a step back, apparently stunned by her appearance. He reeled; then steadied himself, his eyes narrowing as he looked at her.

"Ah know you," he said, carefully studying her face. "You are that Yankee woman, the one who wants to take mah plantation away from me."

"I am Samantha," she replied, fearing what might happen next from this man she barely knew.

"That's right. Samantha," he drawled out her name as if it was a new revelation.

He looked around wildly, apparently dismissing Samantha and suddenly becoming conscious of others standing in the yard. It was as if he looked but did not see.

"Mount up," he commanded. "We will take them this time. Have no mercy!"

Approaching Chase, he continued.

"Are you deaf, man? They're coming in from the west. Hurry!"

"Yes, sir," Chase said in his most military like manner.

Samantha's body shook with fear and amazement. This man who had treated her so badly before the war had completely lost his mind. A wide spectrum of emotion encompassed her body, ranging from compassion to fear. Looking to Chase and Nathan for direction, she followed their lead of not riling him.

"Is he drunk?" Chase whispered to Nathan.

Nathan shook his head.

"I think the war has cost him his mind."

Filled with despair, Grady positioned himself on the front steps of the porch; and with his head in his hands, began to weep uncontrollably. Samantha moved towards him, filled with concern. As she reached out to touch his shoulder in an effort to console him, he flew into a rage once again.

"Evil woman," he cried, "stay away from me! Life was fine until you came to mah beloved south. See what you've done. Mah plantation is in shambles. Nothin' will ever be the same. It's your fault. It was your idea to teach the darkies how to read and write. And now they have freedom...after all I've given them. Ah am ruined."

Samantha took a step backwards as Nathan took a step forward to come to her aid and Grady collapsed once more on the steps, once again enveloped in tears.

Safely out of ear shot, Samantha whispered to Nathan and Chase.

"What shall we do?" she choked with emotion.

"I don't quite know," Chase admitted. "We certainly don't want to agitate him anymore. He is clearly demented...lost his mind."

"Seen too much war," Nathan added. "I've seen similar behavior. But he seems to have some lucid moments as well."

Callie and her family stood huddled together, eyes wide with fear, wondering if an evil spirit had taken over the master of the plantation. Little Hope clung to Izzy's apron in fear.

Suddenly and without warning, Grady was on his feet once again with a wild look in his eyes.

"Did you hear that?" he yelled as he leaped to his feet. "They are coming! Take cover. Rally, men! They mustn't outflank us this time. Get ready boys. Keep your ammunition dry. Keep your heads. We will take them this time!"

Grady was at full alert, gazing down the lane of magnolias, fully believing union troops would come galloping in for battle. He listened intently and then suddenly turned and raced towards his horse. With one outburst of energy, he leaped into the saddle. The horse, startled by the unexpected weight of a rider, reared, pawing the air with his front feet. Grady, not having time to be securely situated in the saddle, slid from it and hit the ground with a thud. The horse snorted and reacted in terror, his front hooves trampling Grady's body. Nathan and Chase both ran towards the accident, Nathan grabbing the reins of the wild-eyed horse to stop the assault and settle him down while Chase bent over the trampled body. Grady moaned with pain as Chase attempted to assess the damage. Samantha ran to his side.

Grady opened his eyes and whispered her name.

"Samantha."

"Hang on, Grady. We will get you help. Don't move," Samantha encouraged.

Blood began to trickle from his mouth and his eyes rolled in his head and his breath came in short gasps. Then his eyes flew open as if there was a moment of clarity.

"The South shall rise again!" he shouted, raising his right arm.

His body slumped in Chase's arms and Grady Reynolds was dead.

23

Washington, D.C.

Nathan stood on the steps of the shambles of apartments, the scrap of paper written in Red's own scrawl clutched tightly in his hand. *1402 Cambridge St.* He checked the address on the paper with the one on the front of the building. This then, must be where Red's little sister, Susanna, must live. Looking around, Nathan felt a twinge of emotion…first for his friend, Red and secondly for the deplorable conditions Red's family must experience. He raised his hand to knock on the door.

"Yes?"

A beautiful young girl opened the door. She had the same red in her brown eyes and the same flaming red hair as Red had. No doubt this was Susanna.

"Susanna?" Nathan asked.

Susanna looked up and down the street and then back at Nathan.

"Who wants to know?"

"My name is Nathan Clevenger. I served in the war with I believe your brother Red."

Susanna was visibly touched by the sound of her brother's name. She moved aside.

"Won't you come in?" she said simply.

Nathan stepped inside the door into a small room that in spite of the outside condition of the building, was remarkably clean.

"It ain't good news, is it?" the girl said.

The muscles in Nathan's stomach contracted and he tried desperately to take a deep breath.

"No," he whispered. "But he asked me to come to tell you personally."

Susanna comprehended what Nathan was trying to tell her and began to cry.

"Glad Maw didn't live to hear the news. She missed him terrible. We all did."

"He cared deeply for you," Nathan offered, gently touching the girl on her shoulder.

She nodded.

"I'd like to tell you what I know about him. He was a good friend to me."

Again she nodded.

Nathan began his narrative and told her all the things he knew about Red, including how brave he was, how much joy he provided in the dismal war camps, and how his last thoughts were of his little sister. It was something that had to be done...for both Susanna...and for Nathan.

"Samantha, it's so good to have you home," Claudia Stewart smiled, placing her delicate hand on Samantha's arm as they sat at the dinner table.

Claudia's cheeks were pink once more in contrast to the paleness of the past few years. Her eyes, which were dark and sunken on Samantha's arrival, now were alive and sparkling with happiness. And having the entire family around the dinner table had left her with the breathless anticipation of happier days. And then there was Nathan who had joined the family for dinner. Just like old times...times before the war.

"I'm glad to be here, too. But more importantly, I am so pleased you are feeling better, mother," Samantha answered.

Sylvester Stewart beamed from the other end of the table, relieved at his wife's improvement in health since Samantha's return.

Samantha patted her mother's hand and smiled sweetly at Nathan who sat across the table from her. Both he and Chase were beginning to resemble the men they had been before the war, appearing well rested and having gained some weight.

Samantha studied the faces at the table, Nathan sitting facing her; although still pale, the light had returned to his eyes and the haggard look had all but disappeared. Chase sat next to Nathan, looking healthier than he had for months, although scars were still visible on his boyish face and he physically winced in pain when he overused his injured shoulder. Samantha felt a twinge of guilt when she saw Chase's scars, realizing the things he suffered was because of her. Clinton's quiet wife was next, a woman Samantha needed to get to know better. Father glowed with pride from his place at the head of the table at having all his family once again gathered in the dining room. A very stodgy Clinton Stewart showed a chink in his otherwise austere appearance when he looked at his newborn son, Sylvester Clinton Stewart. Family names would be passed on to the next generation. The suave Edward, seated on Samantha's right had not lost his boyish appeal…or his appetite.

"Pass the potatoes, please," he asked. "I'm starved."

"You're always starved," Samantha said. "Think about all the men in the war who went without food."

Edward looked directly at Nathan.

"My apologies. It must have been a horrible experience."

Nathan put his fork on his plate and shifted his weight uncomfortably in his chair.

"Worse," he said. "A lot worse."

"Were you ever injured?" Edward continued.

"Several times," Nathan responded. "The injured are moved to the rear, but as soon as they're able, or even before, they are put back on the front lines."

"That's rough," Edward empathized.

"Not as rough as losing a good friend."

He had blurted out the words as if they had been waiting in the wings for the exact cue.

Edward stopped eating and looked closely at Nathan before he responded.

"I'm going to guess many good friends were lost," he said softly.

Nathan nodded his head, at first not being willing to continue.

"I lost Red," he choked.

Silence enveloped the table.

"He was one of my closest friends. A real likeable guy. Had bright red hair."

All eyes were focused on Nathan.

"He died in my arms."

Nathan gave an audible sigh before he continued.

"His father was mostly a drunkard and was never around so Red had taken care of his mother and little sister...a real upstanding guy. One of the last things he did was make me promise to tell his sister."

Again he paused with emotion. He had everyone's attention.

"I found her last week. Not an easy thing to do."

He paused again; and Samantha, feeling his unwillingness to continue, came to his aid.

"I know that must have been difficult for you. But I know you. And you helped her through it. That's possibly a reason for Red choosing you to be the one to talk to his sister. I think that's a great compliment. You are a good friend, a good man."

Nathan's eyes met hers and a feeling of peace came over him. She bolstered him when he was down. He had evidenced that on the long trip back from South Carolina in the many hours of conversations they had shared. Although Samantha had many stimulating qualities, she also possessed some soothing attributes as well.

Samantha suddenly became self-conscious of her glowing tribute to Nathan.

"The war may have been fought with ammunition in the south," Edward continued, "but it was waged in this city as well, perhaps in a little different way. Washington politicians have been fighting their own battles here. Not everyone agreed with the war, you know. Some of us were thrilled with the news of Lee's surrender to Grant, but that piece of good news was quickly devastated by President Lincoln's assassination. It was like one day there were shouts of victory and the next, there was despair."

"Were you close to any of the prominent figures, Edward?" Chase asked.

"Only on the periphery. I dealt with some in the business. But I was with friends in the audience at Ford's Theatre the night of April 14th."

Samantha was shocked.

"I did not know that," she said as she turned towards him, placing her hand on his arm.

"I couldn't see the president from where I was sitting, but I had heard some talk that he was in the audience, heard the shot that echoed through the theatre, the commotion that ensued and observed the confusion and saw Booth as he hit the stage floor and limped away. It was like no one could wrap their minds around the situation enough to grab him. I've heard gun shots before, but this one seemed to penetrate my very being, even before I comprehended what had taken place. It seemed as if it took seconds for anyone to react. The play stopped, of course, and it wasn't long before the news spread that the president had been shot. There was a lot of yelling and pushing and shoving from people trying to get a better look. Typical things people do out of panic and shock."

Edward pushed back emotion as he spoke.

"I stood in the crowd outside Petersen's house with everyone else, hoping for some news, asking anyone who came from the house for information. Then someone came out the front doors of the house and said President Lincoln had only a few hours to live. It wasn't a formal announcement or anything. Just a comment in answer to the inquiries being made as the man made his way down the street. A silence like I've never heard before came over the crowd. No longer was there whispering and questions being asked. Some were praying and then someone started sobbing; and before long, the sound of crying replaced every other sound on the street."

Edward stopped as he relived the events of that fateful evening.

"Lincoln was a great man," Sylvester Stewart volunteered from his place at the head of the table. "A great man. Carried a lot of burden in his presidency."

Clinton concurred, adding his own comment.

"A noble man. But not everyone in Washington would agree with that."

Edward continued.

"At the beginning of the war, Lincoln saw fit to assemble troops to protect the capital city. Soldiers practically overran the town. We experienced all kinds of problems with that influx of men."

"Yes," added Clinton, "Washington has become a place for freed slaves to congregate. People need food and places to stay."

"And, yes, Nate," Edward said softly, "Washington became an area to provide for wounded soldiers."

There was a pause while Nathan reflected on those he knew would need medical attention and Edward and Clinton recalled the desperate look in the faces of those who needed help.

Claudia Stewart interrupted the uncomfortable pause.

"I am really sorry about Grady's death, Samantha, dear. The war is so tragic."

It was Samantha's turn to sigh. Claudia Stewart's life really was one far removed from reality and the tragedy of war. Samantha had skillfully spared everyone except Chase and Nathan the details of Grady's death.

"The war was not kind to anyone and certainly not to Grady, mother. He is finally at peace at his beloved Hummingbird Hill. I think he held on until he made it back so he could die there."

Claudia Stewart shook her head in agreement, apparently satisfied with that explanation while Samantha hoped there was nothing in her tone that would indicate her true feelings about Grady Reynolds.

But Sylvester Stewart heard the evasiveness in his daughter's comments.

"Who wants more biscuits?" Sylvester asked as he picked up the basket and passed them around the table.

"Did I ever tell you the story about how Nathan saved my life and he wasn't even there?" Chase began. "It was a trick he showed me when we were kids and it came to me at the right time."

With that, Chase launched into his story. However, he added some drama to it to make it even more entertaining.

Clinking of china and silverware indicated everyone was once again concentrating on fine dining and a change in conversation.

Not long after the conclusion of dinner, Claudia excused herself to go to her room to rest and Sylvester accompanied his wife.

Clinton gathered his little family to return to their own home and Edward had Chase in deep conversation about something or other.

"Will you accompany me to the veranda, Samantha?" Nathan inquired.

"I would be most honored," she said as she took his arm and they moved into the comfort of the cool summer night.

Stars twinkled overhead and a quarter moon shone against the dark sky. Neither spoke. Nathan leaned his arms on the wrought iron bannister, staring into the night, thoughts of a younger couple who had shared this scene before running through his mind.

"You're awfully quiet," Samantha said softly.

"Just enjoying the evening," he responded.

"Yes, it's a beautiful evening."

She thought for a time.

"South Carolina seems so far away tonight."

"Maybe that's a good thing," he said.

He turned towards her, not failing to notice how the moonlight cast bewitching shadows across her beautiful face.

"We have a lot to forget. We have a lot to remember."

She nodded her head in agreement.

He found her hands.

"Samantha," he whispered, "is it too soon for me to come calling?"

She laughed softly.

"You're here now, aren't you?" she quipped.

"You know what I mean. I want to come to you as your suitor, as more than your friend."

She raised her hands to touch his face.

"You know you are already more than that. You always have been. I was such a fool to be taken in by his..."

Nathan put his fingers to her lips.

"It's okay," he murmured. "That is in the past. It's over. It's unfortunate...just like the war...like all the killing. You have to believe in the future. We have to believe."

"Is there a future?"

"There is a future if you want there to be one. Believing is the only thing that makes a difference."

Nathan's arms stole around her waist.

"I don't want to push you, Samantha," he whispered. "I realize you've been through a lot."

"And you as well," she murmured.

"You deserve more," he offered.

"And I want more," she confided. "I want a life with a home and children and I want to share it with a man I can love and respect."

"I hope I can earn that respect."

"You already have, Nathan. Thoughts of you and your kindnesses to me throughout the years gave me comfort during the really troublesome times."

He laughed in agreement.

"I carried your letter with me through the entire war. It got pretty tattered and dirty and I got teased about it some. But a lot of us had mementoes that kept us sustained during the tough times. I took it out of my cap every night and read it when I was tired and discouraged. It was such a comfort to me."

Her heart overflowed at the thought of her words meaning that much to him.

"And the last line of the letter where you wrote: *Come in the spring of the year. It is particularly lovely here when the magnolias are in bloom.*"

"And they were, Nathan, they were! And you did come in the spring...just like I wanted you to."

"I can't tell you the emotion I felt as I rode through the arches of magnolia trees when I found you."

"Yes, they were particularly lovely," she smiled.

"It was as if they were lighting the way...welcoming me...encouraging me."

"I thought that, too," she said. "Before I even recognized you, the white flowers with their sweet fragrance seemed to glow behind you."

They stood totally lost in each other's eyes. Then hers clouded and she turned from him.

"I saw the look in your eyes the day I was married. It haunted me. I knew I had hurt you deeply and felt so guilty about that."

He gently touched her arm.

"I probably should have expressed what I was feeling, but it seemed to happen so quickly. One day we were kids playing hide and seek and the next thing I knew you were in someone else's arms."

"I'm sorry, Nathan. I am so sorry," she cried.

Tears began to stream from her eyes and he removed the silk handkerchief from his pocket and tenderly wiped them from her face.

"There you go again," she laughed. "Always wiping my tears away."

"I just want to take care of you…to wipe the tears away forever."

"You are the only man who can do that for me. Right from the beginning, I found myself comparing Grady to you…and he always came up lacking. You were never out of my mind."

"Mistakes made. Lessons learned."

She turned to him.

Moonlight streamed down upon them as if they were caught in the spotlight on a stage. The scent of roses wafted from the gardens. Stars winked from their places in a carpet of blue. She rested her head on his shoulder as he enfolded her in his arms. So comfortable, so secure. Slowly the first steps towards recovery were put into place.

The summer of 1865 waned. Although it had been filled with healing of bodies, spirit and emotion, tragedy still remained in the lives of many. The country had begun to heal…from the hatred, from the war, from the effects of the war, from the tragic death of a president, from the growing pains of change, the effects of hundreds of slaves set free, many who had no idea of how to live outside the chains of slavery.

The streets of Washington were somewhat safer than they had been during the war years. The sounds of carriage wheels mingled with the rustling of the trees. A late summer breeze was welcomed after hot and sticky summer days. The lamplighter had just started making his rounds, using the long pole to reach the wicks in the lanterns. It was a magical show to watch them as the lights appeared one by one. Once they were all lit, his task for the evening was completed, but he would return the following morning to extinguish them and clean and repair them for the following evening's display.

"Sometimes I wonder what they're doing," Chase said wistfully.

"Who's that?" Samantha asked.

"Rob and Pa Rice and Oma…all the people who helped me on my journey to find you."

"They are really good people, aren't they?"

"Good people. I even think about what happened to Barnes. I still wonder if he got in trouble for letting me go…or even if he did indeed let me go. I hope he wasn't punished for my escape. I will always think he was a good man, trying to get by just like everyone else in the war. Just wanting to get back to his family."

He sat pensively for several moments as they watched the lamplights come on one by one.

"How about you? Do you think of anyone at the plantation?"

"Oh, yes," Samantha sparked. "And I was pleasantly surprised this week. I received a letter from Izzy. You know, Grady did not want me to teach Izzy how to read and write. But she is such a sweet girl…and smart. And she certainly was devoted to me. They are doing well. Hope is growing like a weed, as Izzy put it. And the best news of all, she is expecting another child."

With that Samantha became overcome with emotion.

"Yes, I miss her. I miss Callie and Elijah as well and their children. But I miss Izzy most of all."

"Here comes the angel," the patient said from his bed.

Upon hearing that news, a second patient lifted himself up on one arm to see the beautiful young woman whose personality had brightened their Wednesdays each week.

"Good morning," she perked. "How are my favorite patients?"

"Better now you're here," a third man chimed in.

"That's what I like to hear," she said as she sat down the tray of bandages and salves she had brought with her. "Who's first?"

She stood with her hands on her hips as they all vied for her attention.

"But," the first soldier said, "you'd better have a look at Scoggins. He had a bad night. I think he might be in trouble."

Samantha's eyes immediately found the cot occupied by Lieutenant Scoggins. Indeed, the lieutenant did not look well at all. Samantha moved to his bed and felt his forehead with the back of her hand. Fever for sure. And then she saw the blood stained sheet as she attempted to straighten it.

"How long has he been like this?" she asked.

"He was that way when I woke up this morning."

"I'll be back," she said as she hurried from the room and down the hallway to locate the first doctor she could find.

To say doctors were overworked and understaffed at the hospital was an understatement. There were so many veterans who needed their attention and volunteers like Samantha Stewart were invaluable to the work. But by the time she returned with the doctor and the laudanum, it was apparent another soldier would be added to the list of casualties. The body was removed from the room as quickly as possible and Samantha went about her weekly chores tending to the others who needed attention. She did her best to keep up a banter of conversation with them, but each time she lost a patient, it was personal with her.

"It's okay, Samantha," the soldier said as she removed his soiled bandages. "You can't save us all."

"I know," she said softly. "But that doesn't take away the desire to try."

"I'm available to take you dancing tonight," he flirted.

The soldier flinched as she removed the part of the bandage that was near the wound.

"Hey, that hurt."

"You'd better behave yourself or this procedure could get a lot worse."

They both laughed and she prepared to move on to the next patient, having applied the salve and wrapped the wound in clean cloth. Even those items were at a premium.

"Thanks, beautiful," he called to her as she washed her hands before starting on the next patient's bandages.

Volunteering at the church that had been converted into a hospital was helpful to the injured. It was helpful for other kinds of healing as well.

It was a warm late summer evening, with storm clouds threatening overhead. Sundays were always a day of rest. The Stewart family enjoyed a late meal after attending church services across town. And Nathan Clevenger was a typical Sunday guest these days. The afternoon had been filled with games of croquet and glasses of lemonade. Samantha had cared for her nephew while his mother relaxed a bit in the sunshine and now Clinton and his family had returned to their own home. Chase was calling on a young lady he had frequently been seeing socially and Samantha and Nathan were sitting on a marble bench near the rose bushes after a stroll through the gardens.

"I'm so very proud of you, Samantha," he said. "Your work at the hospital has been good for you and I'm quite sure the soldiers are happy to have such a gorgeous young lady attending them."

"I do enjoy the work. I like helping people. And not only with their physical problems. Sometimes they just need someone to talk with. This week I wrote a letter for one of the soldiers...a letter home to his mother."

"That's what I mean. You do more than is required of you because you are genuinely concerned about people. You care."

She thought for a moment.

"Maybe too much," she confessed. "When I lose a patient, I really feel so responsible."

"That's a feeling we all have had."

Once again they sat silently, each with their own set of memories of the pain and turmoil they had experienced.

"Will we ever heal from this horrid war?" she asked.

"Time. It will take time. I hope the history books will include the stories of individuals when they write our story. War is so much more than battle lines and generals and political views."

They watched with interest as a bird splashed into one of the fountains and bobbed its head and fluttered its wings in enjoyment.

"I must say, Samantha, you looked totally at home taking care of your nephew this afternoon."

"Thank you," she replied, looking into his sparkling eyes. "Is there further comment on that?"

"No, no," he explained. "I just meant that I enjoyed the picture…you know, you with a baby in your arms."

"Oh," she teased. "You didn't think I was capable. Is that it?"

"Now you are twisting my words," he protested.

She giggled at his sudden uncomfortableness.

"I know what you're saying," she confessed. "It's just that you get this incredible look when you're challenged."

He sat back against the bench.

"Well, Samantha Stewart, you certainly are a challenge. I'll say that for you. But then you always have been. And, come to think of it, it's a challenge I've always enjoyed."

They sat quietly for a time, enjoying the calm of the garden atmosphere, listening to the sounds of end of a season insects, inhaling the fragrance of late blooming flowers.

"See that balcony up there?" Nathan pointed out. "The veranda."

"Yes," she answered. "It's been there my entire life. Nothing new about it."

"It's special," he said.

She turned towards him with a puzzled look on her face.

"Why is a balcony special?" she asked. "Especially one that's been there forever. Why, you and I must have played on that balcony since we were what? Five years old?"

"That's my point," he rallied.

She waited for more.

"That's what makes it so special," he continued. "We've shared so many experiences on that balcony...you and I. Like earlier in the summer when you and I were there after dinner and the stars were so brilliant and the night air was so wonderful. Do you remember that night, Samantha?"

"I remember," she said, seriously.

"I remember something else," she began but hesitated.

Perhaps it was only her memory and not his.

"What do you remember, Samantha?"

"I remember my sixteenth birthday party," she said, shyly. "You were there. We danced. We came to the balcony."

She paused, a little reluctant to go any further, and absently reached for the tiny silver ring on the chain around her neck. The movement did not go unnoticed by Nathan. He slipped his arm around her shoulder.

"Yes, I was at the party and yes, we danced and yes, we came out to the balcony. Was there more to the evening?"

"Well, yes, you gave me my birthday gift. And..."

She suddenly became very shy.

"Well, it was just a very nice evening," she announced, suddenly getting to her feet.

Nathan stood as well, not willing the moment should pass.

"Yes...your birthday gift...the silver ring...and..."

Nathan took Samantha's hands in his.

"Do you remember anything else, Samantha?" he prodded.

She still remembered the tingle his kiss had started in her body. But she avoided his gaze. He gently lifted her chin until their eyes met.

"Samantha," he whispered.

"It was my first kiss," she trembled.

He had always thought she was the most remarkable and most beautiful woman alive and now, as his arms closed around her, he shivered with emotion.

"But not your last kiss," he whispered as his lips met hers.

The emotion of that first kiss was only surpassed by another.

"Samantha," Nathan whispered, "the image of you with the baby in your arms is one I want to fulfill with our children. I have loved you as long as I can remember breathing. You sustain me. You give me hope. You complete me. Will you marry me?"

"Yes. Yes, Nathan," she breathed.

Clouds that had threatened earlier dissipated to allow the moon to shine down upon them. Stars winked in the sky. A refreshing breeze swept through the gardens as love swept through their hearts.

The past was the past and some of it would be debated for years to come. But the future lay ahead of them, promising healing and happiness. And believing is the thing that makes the difference.

The End

Books by G.L. Gracie

Amelia

The Rose Trilogy:

Ivy and Wild Roses

Sweet Primrose

The White Rose

Willow

Refuge from the Storm

When Magnolias Bloom

G.L. Gracie has been writing since she was thirteen years old, creating short stories, plays and poetry. Now she is developing novels. She is the mother of three and lives in southwestern lower Michigan. She likes to build her characters around the simple things of life, those things that form us and make us what we are.

CPSIA information can be obtained
at www.ICGtesting.com
Printed in the USA
FFOW02n1643291115
19098FF